CORNUCOPIA

CORNUCOPIA

For Jess.

My love, my life, and my light in this occasionally dark yet beautiful world.
My matching Tetris piece.
My yellow Wellington boots during the rain.
My emotional blanket fort.

"Understand, I'll slip quietly
away from the noisy crowd
when I see the pale stars rising, blooming, over the oaks.

I'll pursue solitary pathways
through the pale twilit meadows,
with only this one dream:

You come too."

Rainer Maria Rilke

....

Also, for James.

Thank you for the support and help.

You were the one to give me the fire to write this story, my first.

For that, you have my everlasting thanks.

....

DISCLAIMER

This is a work of fiction. Names, characters, businesses, events, and incidents are purely the products of the author's imagination. Any resemblance to actual persons, living or dead, or events is purely coincidental.

TRIGGER WARNINGS

Printed on the following page is a short list naming the subjects involved in this novel that some readers may find disturbing and/or triggering.

They may contain minor spoilers for the story ahead, but the author would much rather you know these and feel comfortable going forward.

This book occasionally contains horror scenes as well as other troubling aspects.

Such is life.

TRIGGER WARNINGS

This book contains instances of Drug misuse, kidnapping, suicide, gore, animal abuse, and torture.

CORNUCOPIA

Prologue : Mother's Ruin

The city horizon.

A sight that is beautiful to some. To the hundreds and thousands of hazy-eyed tourists incoming every hour and every day.

Here for a weekend of booze, slot machines and hedonism. Shotgun weddings and instant divorces are together a part of the all-inclusive package.

A skyline of high-rise buildings flash spectrums of colours that dance across the sky; forever pulsating with life and energy.

To her, the town is a muted hollow.

An empty, shallow valley of sorrow.

It was her that had changed; not the place.

The city remained the same, always.

A city that never sleeps.

A vista of neon lights advertised all manners of delights: Dancers, Karaoke, Cheap Drinks, Now Performing: That Band that you can't remember the name of but had a Top 10 hit in the late 1970s.

Every day.

Every moment.

24/7 - 365.

CORNUCOPIA

To the tourists it is an opportunity for joy, escape, freedom and depravity. A weekend of slot machines and strippers; ice-cold vodka sipped and cocaine snorted in mirrored back rooms.

To her, it is a pallid and empty depthless pit of a place that contained her despair.

A pulsating and never-ending assault to her senses that battered her soul into submission and oblivion.

It had been two years.

Two long and agonising years.

Seven hundred and thirty-one days, to be precise.

Seven hundred and thirty-one days of pain and suffering.

The police hardly took notice back in the beginning.

She hoped they would take notice now.

She recalled memories deep in the recesses of her mind and began to cry sobs from the depths of her soul.

Two years ago.

Her son.

Her only son.

Missing and never found.

"This kind of thing happens all the time", the police said.

"Give it a few days. He'll turn up."

He didn't.

Weeks followed.

Pictures were put on local notice boards and cardboard milk cartons.

LOST.

IF SEEN PLEASE CONTACT...

Nothing.

Not a single drop of information.

"We've used all of our resources", they said.

"Doors have been knocked. CCTV has been surveilled. There's nothing."

It was on the local TV channels for a day or two before he was forgotten by someone or something else.

Another tragedy.

A momentary fraction of guilt seeped into her psyche as she couldn't remember who replaced her son in the news. She imagined the feelings of grief felt by so many around her, and yet the city never changes.

It never stops. An endless vortex of other people's pleasure and hedonism surrounded her, it encapsulated her desperation and grief.

CORNUCOPIA

She gnawed at her fading and chipped nail varnish; a damp light coral pink; she replays the past within her memory.

"Sometimes people just don't want to be found. Especially here."

She remembers his perfect face.

His dimpled cheeks were mixed deeply with freckles that speckled across his brow.

He had bright and crystalline blue eyes; piercing and luminous with a young and unrestrained spirit.

He bore a smile; wide and joyful, he had a soul that brimmed with childlike wonder, full of love and hope.

He had strawberry blonde hair with a streak of whatever his favourite colour was that month.

Her favourite was a pale and earthy bottle green, so this is what she remembered.

Skinny as a beanpole; she remembers her fingers being as tiny and wide as his; they wore each other's jewellery after too many sips of wine late at night.

They have lived here since his father passed away twenty-two years ago.

He was six years old; confused about where his father was and why the cancer had suddenly taken him to heaven so quickly.

Ever since then, they lived here together, closer than birds of a feather.

They shared every single intimate detail with one another.

How work was the night before; the gossip of the bar and shop floors, the talk of the town. The drunks, the low-lives, the high-rollers and the men in well-fitted suits that had flirted with them.

She is a bartender, and he is a card dealer. Both merchants of vice; they were not proud of their jobs, but they had to do what they could to survive.

She reaches into her handbag and her fingers momentarily caressed the cold and loaded .380 Ruger LCP.

She felt herself move the safety switch to the OFF position; it released a low and unmistakable click.

She found her pack of almost depleted Lucky Strike Reds and removed one. She put it in her trembling mouth, marking it with bright red lipstick.

She remembers infinite nights reaching into the early dawn that were full of laughter, booze, and cigarette smoke. All spent with her one and only baby boy. They watched movies, ate popcorn, and danced to their favourite songs in their barely furnished kitchen; empty bottles of wine littering the countertops. Together, their feelings were shared; their hearts mingled and spirits entwined. It was a strange love, but it was theirs.

She put her hand into her pocket and pulled out a weathered silver hip flask; it was a gift she got from work for her 50th Birthday; this was the first time she had used it. Unscrewing the lid, a smell of ethanol and juniper permeated her nostrils.

A solid gulp of hot alcohol was followed by a body-wide shudder of disgust; a burning fire lit in her belly. Retching at the taste of it, she unceremoniously dumped the remnants of the flask over the desert hilltop as she searched out the item that was now the only thing that remained of her son, hidden in her petite leather handbag.

A matchbook with one remaining within it. Removing the cardboard envelope from her bag, she lit the final match against the blue-coloured strike patch.

The flame quivered in the breeze as she brought it up quickly to the end of the coffin nail that nestled in between her lips.

The cigarette now lit, and she took her first pull.

The red embers of burning tobacco matched the lights from the city. Smoke mingled and rose with the light haze of fog in the air.

As she flicked the used shard of wood into the dusty distance she looked at the matchbook for one last time.

A now faded pale coral blue paper with gaudy writing stated, "Vincenzos Famous Bar & Grill."

On the back; the beginnings of a series of numbers had been written hastily; the middle and end of the digits had been torn out.

As well as this, her son's last words to her, written in tightly bunched, hurried and intoxicated cursive.

"I'm here. Back Soon. Michael. XxXxX."

In the days following Michael didn't r, she reported it to the authorities. She even showed them his message, written in Michael's hand.

"Ma'am, we are doing everything we can."

They weren't.

CORNUCOPIA

After weeks of asking it was time to take things into her own hands.

She remembers visiting the establishment, questioning customers and bartenders about the evening. She continually and perpetually drew blanks. By the state of the bar and staff, it wasn't surprising that the people would want to forget everything that happened within its walls.

And so day after day, week after week, month after month, she despaired. Ever questioning, never receiving answers.

The hilltop she now stood on was the first view she and her son saw of the city when they moved here. Back at that moment many years ago, it was a feeling of opportunity and growth tinged with the desperation of having to make things work for both of them. She was determined to be a good mother. To always be there. To always love and care. To always protect.

A cold wind blew her back to reality, returning her to the ashen picture of the smog lingering skyline.

Her hands shook with the combination of delirium tremens, nicotine and terror, a cold wind blew the now extinguished cigarette out of her fingers and across the rocky sand-strewn plane.

Looking at her surroundings, she spotted a small rock, and carefully buried the matchbook beneath it.

She took the gun out of her purse slowly, full of reverence. It lay heavy and weighted in her hand.

She saw the box of bullets in her purse, now half empty.

CORNUCOPIA

Hollow points.

One shot.

One kill.

She placed the gun in her mouth, the metal scraped against her teeth.

The last sensation to move through her was the taste of cold steel, tears and sweat from her brow.

She muttered a short prayer and pulled the trigger.

Her blood and skull splattered across the hilltop, sending shards of bone and blood into the desert sand.

The faint music from the city never ceased, not even for the lightest of moments.

Sirens flew across the city, but they were not for her.

They were for someone else in the city that never sleeps.

CORNUCOPIA

Chapter 1 - Paradise Lost

Another long night shift ends.

Another trawling, bleak night of stacking chips and passing rigged hands. Another night of dollar bills exchanged for hope, another night of ripping the ordinary people off their hard-earned money, all for their attempt at redemption. For the people, it was another rush of adrenaline, another turn of the cards provided by the cruel gods of luck; endlessly enticing, ever watchful, ever eager for another twist of fate, always hungry for another cosmic coin flip.

For Michael, it was just an occupation—a stop-gap job that had turned into a two year long career and counting.

Michael wasn't proud of his job, but he was good at it. He effortlessly spread cards, chips, and dollar bills into the casino bank, an endless chasm of fortune, always hungry for more. A depthless pit, ready to accept the coins of the desperate. Ready to receive the sacrifice of the willing.

At the end of his 10-hour shift, full of curse words, momentary joyous celebrations, and a couple of spilt drinks, he vividly remembers walking towards home, the familiar route. Another evening fading into the next day. It was the end of the week at work for him, a long series of early afternoons leading into late evenings, smoky, sweaty, and drawling. His routine at the end of a Sunday evening, the beginning of his weekend, was always to have a few drinks somewhere before heading home with 2 Chinese meals and some cheap bottles of wine for his Mom.

The standard order would be a cheap, room temperature Chardonnay, and potentially a bottle of Riesling matched alongside Yangzhou Rice, Red Pork dumplings, a side order of Crab Rangoon all tied up with the obligatory fortune cookies. Last week's sweet biscuits read, "If you want the rainbow, you must tolerate the downpour. Your lucky numbers are 16 & 53" & "Nothing is impossible to a willing heart. Your lucky numbers are 45 & 97."

The sheer amount of bars open at all hours along his usual walk were metaphorically countless; they idled endlessly along the strip, selling their produce of pleasure and recreation until the early morning hours. An ever-present reminder that the town's main export was hangovers, regret, and empty pockets.

On one occasion many moons ago, he thought he would make a game of it. At the end of his week, he would go into the next bar neighbouring the one he visited the previous time. All counting towards the time until he had completed the circuit of bars, backrooms, and dives, the last one being the closest to home. This would be sometime in the distant future, but fate had different plans for him.

Tonight, he meandered into a place he wouldn't usually stay in for long. A small and shabby area in the middle of a haze of others, adjacent to a trash-filled alleyway of rusted fire escapes, leftover bent brown spoons, and sharp rusted needles.

Vincenzo's Bar & Grill.

It was the kind of place where your shoes stuck to the floor if you stood still for more than a few seconds. A stagnant station of hot and sweaty beginnings, full of cold and foetid endings. It was the kind of place where you could tell everyone was taking at least one type of white powder or coloured pill, if not several. Half-full tumblers of dark liquor littered the decrepit wooden tables, and a tattered and torn pool table stood in the smoky distance, empty of balls, splintered cues perched in their cracked plastic nests. Glassy-eyed patrons leered into the abyss, infested deeply within the blur of the bar.

CORNUCOPIA

The music and atmosphere were what he would usually avoid, a loud haze of annoying electronic twangs piercing his restrained and fragile eardrums. The drawl of drunken dialogue cascaded a familiar drone of public intoxicated conversation, crawling, cantankerous and cataclysmic. A foggy, hot, and perspiring pit of gloom. The epitome of a dive.

The bartender, however, was exactly his type. When he laid eyes on him, he thought to himself, "I owe the game at least one drink here."

And so he approached the vast oaken precipice strewn with metal towers that drooped with dripping beer nozzles, spirit bottles lay hidden in the damp speed rail underneath, unwashed and speckled with mildew.

The barkeep stood wide, muscular, and defined; his haircut was sculpted into a sharpened and deliberate undercut, it swept to the side with a sweat-moistened flourish. Flecks of grey lay amid a sea of thick amber-brown hair while a perfectly groomed short beard shrouded his plump, full lips.
He served the waiting patrons with fluid grace and ease, performing quick, colourful spins before pouring liquid into highball glasses with twirling effortlessness.

Michael nervously walked up and waited patiently to order his usual.

After a while, the broad figure made eye contact with him; his eyes were a pure vibrant green as bright as freshly cut grass; as stunning as raw, unrefined jade.

Michael nervously coughed his order over the roar of the music.

"A 7&7 with some mint on top, if you have it, please and thank you."

"Sure thing, handsome."

Michael's cheeks flared a rosy red blush of embarrassment. He was not used to being flirted with.

Michael quickly grabbed a matchbook from a black plastic holster on the bartop and wrestled his cigarette box from his pocket before lighting one to hide his ruffled complexion and flustered nerves.

The drink was soon placed in front of him on a small paper napkin; it was wet and creased as it nestled against the wooden steel-laced bar top.

Picking up the icy cold drink, he took a pull from the straw and tasted what was very obviously an extra strong measure.

Feeling the fluid enter his stomach, he glanced down and saw the damp napkin was hiding a message.

It read: "Drink is on me. I finish in half an hour. Stay if you want to; leave if you don't. XxXxX"; the handwriting was dark and deliberate.

And so began a night longer than anticipated.

He had two more drinks while he waited for the unnamed bartender to finish his shift.

Half an hour later Michael saw the man remove his shirt behind the bar; he sprayed himself down with fragrant antiperspirant that smelled of ice and menthol. His body was chiselled, muscular, and perfect. Michael's heart fluttered as he watched the bartender put on a fresh t-shirt and took his first step of the night onto the other side of the bar; his shift was now finished.

For hours, they shared shots, smokes, and stories; their conversation effortlessly ebbed and flowed. They talked about regulars, strangers, and reprobates on a table that creaked and leaned, no matter how many bar coasters were put underneath the feet of the rancid furniture.

They spoke about music, films, and what they liked about each other. They talked about their broken families and wept together. They brought themselves closer to one another slowly until they ultimately kissed under the dim light of a shadowy corner booth.

Michael's body felt like it was lit by a thousand tiny fireflies swarming over his skin in a beautiful sparkling joy. The loud music echoed through his innards, the bass thundering through his ankles, calves, and hips. He tasted bourbon whiskey on his partner's palate; it was earthy, peppery and perfectly warm.

Face to face, mouth to mouth, soul to soul gyrating against each other, writhing flesh colliding together, entwining movements were merged in absolute rhythm and love.

By 3 o'clock, Michael was starting to feel woozy. The booze was hitting him harder than usual, and the clouds of judgement began to form around him. He wanted the night to continue, but he needed to go home, rest, and sleep; but most of all, he needed a shower. His musk from the 10-hour shift grated across him, and he smelt his funk from his glands expanding. It was time to go home. He walked across the thundering dance floor back to his adonis in waiting.

The bartender was sitting as still as a statue in the corner booth, looking at him passionately with eager "Come hither" eyes.

Michael knew he could sense his anxiousness as he began to say his farewell.

Before he could speak, the man who had stolen his heart said softly over the music which was now beginning to quieten as the evening drew to a conclusion.

"It's ok, baby. I'll be around all night. There's no pressure. I'll be down the side alley door. I'll even write the number down to speak to get in. It can be our little secret place."

He tore a piece of cardboard from Michael's matchbook and wrote upon it a series of digits in delightful cursive.

3. 6. 9. 12.

The bartender plucked from his pocket a vial. It was a tiny liquid container, complete with a petite pipette, it was full of what cloudy silver luminous liquid. He squeezed flirtatiously on the rubber nipple and withdrew the nozzle.

Licking his lips in anticipation, he dropped 2 fluid teardrops onto the torn cardboard and lay it on his luscious tongue. He then invited Michael for a goodnight kiss.

"Just remember. 3. 6. 9. 12. Say this at the door, and you'll be welcomed with open arms."

They embraced; their tongues entwined and knotted into one another.

His body ached him to stay and to remain in this Eden, to participate more in this paradise.

He weighed his options until, in the end, a decision was made in his mind. The best of both worlds. He'd go home, shower, change, and head back. What he didn't know was that this would be the last time he'd ever see home.

3. 6. 9. 12.

He walked with purpose, stepping along the sidewalks for a hundred or so minutes, onwards to a brutalist series of apartments.

Clicking his key into the lock furtively, he opened the door and saw the lights were out. His Mom wasn't home yet. He hurriedly stripped, showered, and shaved. He sprayed himself down in his favourite cologne; full of the scent of cedar, geranium, and patchouli.

3. 6. 9. 12.

While putting on fresh clothes, he began to feel the world shift. It began to vibrate, to glow, to expand. The booze and the drugs were starting to hit him. He felt the night's pull drawing him back to where he once was—a tug into the world of excess and passion.

3. 6. 9. 12.

Hurriedly, he wrote a message on the torn matchbook.

"I'm here. Back soon. Michael. XxXxX"

As he stepped out of the door, he locked the door twice. He took a few steps onwards, and in his haze, he forgot himself. He stepped backwards to double-check that he had secured the door. The chemicals that swam in his bloodstream were almost entirely in control of him now. His ankles and heels felt lighter than air as he walked into the night. The brimming lights of the sidewalk proceeded to split, tremoring into shards of palpating ardour and endless spirit.

3. 6. 9. 12.

Michael remembers time passing; back toward his haven of passion, he walked toward a dark side passageway next to the bar, now empty of sound, light, and life.

"3. 6. 9. 12." He called out into a withdrawn slot in a solid steel door.

It opened, and beyond it was a flare of heavenly light, bringing a flood of goosebumps and adrenaline.

Gentle music twinkled from the endless corridor in a soft and pulsating vibrance.

"There's a room where the light can't find you...
Holding hands as the walls keep tumblin' down..."

Something sudden, rough, and violent covered his mouth.

It was not a soft embrace.

It was a harshly made soaking wet cloth; it seemed to vapour; it smelt of sweet ether and pine.

Silver clouds quickly approached his nostrils and fogged his vision as he fell into a depthless pit within his mind.

And after that, darkness.

Darkness for the longest time.

Chapter 2: The Pit & The Pendulum

Michael Young awoke in the pitch-black room.

The smell of ammonia and damp iron from the urine and blood-soaked mattress was now an all too familiar scene to arise to.

He was naked, shivering, and gaunt.

A set of steel shackles chained him to the corner of the room that he was in.

It was long enough so that he could reach all corners of the room but not long enough so that he could touch the door that was sunk into an alcove on the opposite side of his prison.

Even if he could, escape was impossible; the door was thick and solid metal; it guarded against his liberation, a silent and steel-covered sentinel.

A strip light above him turned on, flickering momentarily, and then became steady. It hummed with a soft buzz that sounded like a trapped mosquito.

In one corner, a filth-ridden metal bucket had been recently emptied, but was still foetid and rotten with the smell of human waste.

In the second corner was his bed.

The word "bed" was far too generous a statement.

It is a small single mattress, wrecked with twisting rusted metal springs that sprouted through the ruined fabric like flowers reaching for the sun.

It was deeply stained with blood, his own from the early days of escape attempts.

In the first few days here, he jolted and pulled against his irons, tearing into his flesh, cutting between his veiny wrists, breaking bones, and severing ligaments in a fury of anger.

In the following weeks, he fell into deep wracking tears. Thoughts of who could do this flashed in his mind but always drew a blank.

No one he knew could be this evil or depraved.

He refused to eat for five days in protest to his hidden captors until the temptation became too much for him to bear.

For a while, he cursed and yelled into the empty silence, begging for release, pleading for his life.

For the past year, he resolved himself to the banality of his now empty existence.

Day after day, week after week, he left scratches with his chipped fingernails into the walls of his enclosure, marking the endless days since his capture.

He once held onto the false promise that he might someday have solace. One night, he would be free and go back to his day-to-day routine.

This feeling had long since dispersed; the morbid acknowledgement of his mortality now replaced it.

In the third corner was another bucket.

This one was clean and was packed almost to the brim with water.

CORNUCOPIA

Placed carefully next to it was a single green apple.

Michael saw the bright emerald-coloured fruit and immediately attempted to run over to it.

However young and fit he once was, he certainly wasn't now. He is broken, half-starved, malnourished and suffering from rickets.

He instead crawled on his sunken belly, using his aching, agonised limbs to inch towards it.

As he grasped it, he gnawed at its juicy flesh; its crisp and sweet taste sent waves of pleasure throughout his decrepit being.

The first piece of fresh fruit in two years. A perfect green gem, enlightening his spirit.

His daily rations were always 3 standard MREs.

Freeze-dried mashed potato, hard-tack biscuits with peanut butter, and pill-based supplements.

He did not know what had changed today or why he was given a reprieve, but he wasn't about to question it.

He ate the outside flesh first and then began to eat the core itself. It was crunchy, juicy, and perfectly ripe.

A momentary flash of bliss in this empty husk of a human shell returned the faintest shred of hope to his soul.

It didn't last long.

The light in the room went out.

CORNUCOPIA

He was thrown back into the darkness.

He tried to shout, but only a thin and empty crackle of noise escaped.

It had been so long since he used his voice; it was another shrivelled and withered muscle that made up the empty carcass of his flesh.

A cacophony of ear-ringing thuds swept across the room from above him; he looked up and saw the roof was moving across.

Slowly.

Rhythmically.

He could faintly see the sight of flame, stone, and steel from behind and above the sliding roof.

A towering pillar of brick held dozens of candles, each faintly flickering. It must have been at least 50 feet tall, rising above him.

He heard a low swooping noise. It was like a distant, violent tidal wave, a force of nature that seeped full of power and destruction. A set of candles in the distance were snuffed out, releasing a momentary eruption of smoke that cascaded upwards into the air.

The solid steel door in front of him opened slowly with a heavy thunk.

A tall and wide figure draped in a dark purple gown with a hood thrown over their heads; their face was held in total darkness.

They held in their hand a newspaper clipping.

Michael could see this person's fat fist crumpling the page; each finger was ordained with intricate ornate golden rings and deeply speckled with wispy whitened hair and liver spots.

Michael inched closer.

The towering figure in the doorway threw the sheaf to the floor; it slowly fluttered to the ground. The figure moved backwards and slammed the steel door closed.

Followed by this, a heavy thud of bars lowering and locks clicked into place. Michael was trapped again once more.

Another low swoop, this time closer. It sounded like a gigantic bird of prey flying closer to its target, inching ever closer for the kill. A set of candles closer to him were extinguished in a shadowy puff of smoke.

Michael picked up the piece of newspaper and read.

Several articles were spread around the page, but one was circled with what looked to be ruby-red lipstick. It was the same shade that his mother wore.

The article was an obituary.

"Naomi Young (nee Langton) - Found dead on the outskirts of the city; 07/15/2004. Police are now asking anyone with further information leading to this case to contact them at the local branch, located next to city hall."

Michael collapsed in a heap as tears fell from his eyes.

He attempted again to scream in anguish, but his ragged voice did not comply. The only thing that emerged was a soft and crumbling single word.

"Mom"

A representative from the other side of the door began to speak.

It was a language he did not comprehend; it sounded ancient, strenuous, and warped. It was full of malice, anger, and ill content.

Another swoop from above, he could see now descending closer towards him was a swinging instrument of death.

A shimmering razor-sharp blade several feet long, inching closer and closer to him with every swing.

The voice outside stopped momentarily before resuming shortly after.

This time, the language sounded vaguely familiar.

It was Latin.

"Egestas a Domino in domo impii habitacula autem iustorum benedicentur.
Inlusores ipse deludet et mansuetis dabit gratiam.
Gloriam sapientes possidebunt stultorum exaltatio ignominia,"

Michael attempted again to cry out. A feeble whisper exited his lips.

"Please. What do you want? Just please let me go."

A heavy breeze brushed through Michael's hair as the arcing sweep of the blade chopped the nearest set of candles down the centre, inching him closer to the darkness of death.

The voice, now filled with bile and hatred, spoke in the common tongue. It was screaming at the top of their lungs.

"So shall it be at the end of the world: the angels shall come forth and sever the wicked from among the just. They shall cast them into the furnace of fire: there shall be wailing and gnashing of teeth."

The final push. The last descent.

The blade swept through Michael, entering his ribcage.

It splintered and shattered, slamming his bones and blood against the walls of the small room.

"Momma"

Michael gurgled his last word. Full of harrowing sorrow and death.

Outside the room, the figure threw back their hood and muttered a silent prayer as they swayed, their mind deeply rooted in the verses of power.

Their face was covered in an ivory white mask that covered their eyes, nose, and mouth. It was unmarked, pearlescent, and pure.

They opened their eyes, sallow, bloodshot, and pale.

They unlocked the steel door and surveyed their work.

Nodding to themselves, they slowly reached into the sleeve of their robe and produced a rose.

A bright crimson Centifolia.

CORNUCOPIA

“Hail our Mother, full of grace. By the offering of two bloods, one pure, one tainted, I implore unto you. Bring this world new life. Soon, the sixth seal will be opened, and there shall be a great earthquake. The sun will turn black like a sackcloth made of goat hair. As dust we are, and unto dust we will return.”

They jabbed their finger on a thorn and removed two petals from its crown.

They smeared their blood onto their mask methodically, full of care and compliance.

An ancient sigil, a line of reverence, a sign of their holy faith.

Deep in a trance, the verses and scripture danced through their mind. They stepped towards one half of the cleaved body, still twitching, nerve endings still reacting in two ichorous puddles.

They placed the first rose petal on Michael's closed eyelid.

They now stepped across the corpse, currently laid out in two pieces, as they hummed to themselves a melody of music from Mahler's Kindertotenlieder.

They found themselves at the other half of Michael's body, which was now lying still and lifeless.

They lowered the open eyelid on the body and placed the other rose petal across it.
They spoke a short phrase in hushed, reverent tones, full of passion and fever.

"This too shall pass."

CORNUCOPIA

The masked and hooded figure moved through the door before locking it and flipping off a switch; it extinguished any trace of light in the small blood-filled enclosure.

The endless darkness of the pit fell once more.

Chapter 3: To Protect And Serve

"Welcome to TRGS - the Valley's number one station as voted by YOU. Three years, the champions....."

A short insert of the chorus from a weathered rock song from the 70's cut through the promo.

" THE REAL GREATEST STATION....."

A sound effect of fireworks volleyed through the car's tinny stereo system.

"Playing 24 hours throughout the valley, throughout the city, and WORLD WORLD WORLDWIDE........"

Phoney laser noises pew-pew-pewed, and synthetic fireworks exploded, whirring into the artificial sky.

"Simply the best from the swingin' '60s, the sizzlin' 70's, the heart-achin' 80's, the naughty 90's and MORE!

TRGS.....S.....S.....S......"

A family-friendly jangling of a familiar guitar hook alongside electric fake drums soaked into the ancient Chevy

“Welcome to your life...
There's no turning back...”

The radio was quickly turned off.

"Fucking hate that song"

David Garston made his way at just below 45 KM an hour down the familiar winding city streets. He passed the whore houses, the casinos, the speak-easies, dives and trend-driven night spots that were just beginning to light their advertising bulbs for the heavy day of business ahead.

A slow and silent raincloud loomed overhead; it promised a downpour later on that would make the fresh-faced visitors of the city transform into drowned rats that scurry away from thunder.

He made a left turn onto a cracked and broken road. Looming up ahead of him came the daily sight of a high-rise brutalist concrete fortress that is Police Headquarters. Lady Justice stood high on top, an alabaster warden, ever watchful with blindfolded eyes and weighted fists holding the scales of right and wrong.

Wiping the crusted sleep from the corner of his eyes, he let loose a defeated sigh full of the smell of stale coffee from this morning and bourbon whisky from the night before.

"Another day, another dollar."

David had always wanted to join the service since his favourite uncle bought him a plastic pedal car adorned with police stickers as his fifth birthday present. For three summers until he could no longer fit into it, he rode everywhere, tearing down the suburban streets filled with white picket fences and single-story accommodations that each flew pristinely starched star-spangled banners.

In his youth, he pretended to arrest the older neighbourhood kids for various "crimes" - skipping detention, leaving the house whilst grounded, for kicking a can too loudly down the peaceful streets.

This inevitably led to him being ridiculed and beaten regularly by his peers, but throughout this, he always had a ready and correct sense of justice. A strict and strenuous feeling of fighting the good fight. He was the underdog, but he knew sometime in the future that every dog gets his day.

As soon as he graduated high school he applied for his nearest station. He trained for months; blood, sweat and tears covering his résumé. He was accepted on his first attempt and with flying colours. His parents were so proud, but not as proud as he was of himself. His lifelong dream was achieved gloriously.

He worked his way quickly through the ranks from Technician and Patrol, Vice and Criminal activities, to where he was now: Investigative Homicide Officer. It wasn't a job to be enjoyed. It was a job that was necessary. It was a dirty job that someone had to do; he was the one to do it.

He pulled into the underground car park, a broad and cavernous labyrinth of white lines, concrete and closed circuit cameras. He found his usual space and parked with lacklustre abandon.

Opening the door and exiting the vehicle, his legs released a painful creak, weathered from years of walking the beat. Slamming the door of the heap of a car, he ambled up towards the elevator door, beep-beeping his electric car key in his pocket.

He didn't need to press the elevator button; the door opened as he approached. The night shift would be just finishing now, tired and blackened eyes fluttering desperately for the peace of sleep. Silent nods of acknowledgement, an occasional "Good Morning" mingled with desperate shuffles towards the exit.

He entered the elevator and pressed the number "5"; its digit was worn down from years of thumbs and fingers pushing it. An energetic and cheerful-sounding chime rang as he began his ascent in the narrow steel box.

After a minute or so, the door opened.

CORNUCOPIA

The bullpen was buzzing with activity, as always. Dozens upon dozens of officers answering phone calls, tapping away on keyboards, walking briskly with papers in their hands. Monitors softly flickered as fingers galloped and pecked at keyboards, clacking electronic script onto the displays.

Breathing a deep sigh, he said gently to himself, "First things first".

He wandered over to the break room, a mediocre space of well-worn sofas, fraying magazines that hadn't been replaced in years, an ancient fridge, an old and mouldy microwave and 3 vending machines, idly humming to themselves quietly.

He placed a large cardboard cup on an appliance, which stated "Hot Drinks" in a retro 50's diner-style font. He pressed a plastic button on the machine. ESPRESSO. He pushed it again and then a third time. He pressed another button, "Cold Water". The device thrummed with confusion briefly before sputtering out icy-cold liquid. He grabbed a tiny pot of creamer from the communal fridge, opened the foil lid and dumped it in the cup. He gave it a stir with a fragile wooden stick that was once enveloped in a flimsy paper sheath; he threw it away on the side carelessly. Picking the cup upwards to his awaiting lips, he swallowed a huge gulp, and in one mouthful, the cup was half empty.

Exiting the room, he walked to his desk, sat at the orthopaedic lumbar support chair and pressed the grey and dusty "Power On" button for his screen. He typed in a series of mixed characters and numbers and pressed ENTER.

The computer screen showed a pixelated egg timer, slowly rotating as the hard drive whirred into action.

Looking at his workload of papers, he saw 3 follow-up on reports from yesterday. A hit and run, a domestic assault, a break-in, all needing to be typed, filed and completed. As well as that, there was an off-coral blue paper folder, signalling a new case for inspection. Stuck to the top was a Post-it. "See me for further information. Capt."

Intrigued by this, he picked up the folder and walked through the mingling crowd of black outfits and golden stars to the captain's office.

The blind shutters of the room were half drawn, but he could see his superior officer typing away on her computer, her office phone resting between her ear and neck, craning over, struggling to listen to the voice on the other end. Her reading glasses were perched precariously on the end of her nose.

He knocked.

"Come in."

Her voice held a shallow twang of a restrained Southern sand belt accent; it had been unsuccessfully corrected to sound less rural.

He opened the door and saw his Captain look up from her screen; she peered into his eyes and held up a single skinny finger, indicating, "Give me a minute".

David closed the door carefully; it gave a quiet "click".

Captain Terri Cauldwell, a woman in her mid-forties with glassy blue eyes and a sandy blonde hair tied up in a tight ponytail, wore a pristinely brushed and pressed suit. She was the definition of a perfect leader. It had taken her 10 years to get to this role as Captain; it was not without heartache, betrayal and sexism. She had surpassed this with grace and utmost professionalism under pressure. Steely, solid and strong, she is a born authority, highly organised, motivated and driven for success. Beyond anything, she would do anything for her team.

She sat, whilst still keeping eye contact with David, responding to the phone with an occasional "Uh huh…Yeah for sure...yes of course…No, absolutely not…" to whoever was on the other end of the line. Someone important.

"OK, I have to go now. One of my men is here to see me...yes… yes, of course, I will be in contact again shortly...OK..."

CLICK; the receiver fell back into its black plastic nest.

She huffed in momentary protest as she rubbed her temples and rolled her eyes.

"David. My apologies. That was the DA. You know how he is. Take a seat."

He nodded and complied with the request. He knew precisely how the DA could be.

Lee Harper, District Attorney of the county had been in control of the position for as long as David could remember. An ancient man, he was frail; yet at his peak he would have been as powerful and intimidating as a Kodiak bear. Before he took the bar exam, he was a collegiate offensive lineman on the football team; he was ruthless, aggressive and single-minded. In the last quarter of a game against their rival side, a younger player took a lunging head first tackle at his right leg; with one careless offensive movement, his career was over in a heartbeat; his kneecap had exploded and was now useless.

Full of bitterness, Lee Harper sued the player who had ended his dream of a career in professional sports; and had won. Thus began a new chapter of his life's book. Enlightened by the court's proceedings, beguiled by the terms of reference and intellect, he sank away his muscles, concentrating instead on cerebral workouts and verbal repetitions. Within six years, he had passed a law degree and worked towards the bar examination. He began his new career by working as an appointed attorney for the accused who could not afford public representation. By one way or another, by hook or by crook, he worked his way to his position now: the District Attorney.

David viewed him as a thorn in the police's side, a fly in the ointment, an unnecessary obstacle in the operation. He was endlessly questioning Davids and his team's code of conduct, all for correct procedure. As much as he hated it, he knew that it was the way the system worked. It was how the world spun; fighting against it would be useless. And so he carried on. Nodding the obligatory “Yes Sir”, shaking the compulsory “No Sir”, agreeing the “Three fucking bags full Sir” at court appearances, all to coddle the government and its ancient ways.

The Captain removed her glasses as she made solid, unblinking eye contact with David sitting in front of her.

"Have you read the report?"

"No, Ma'am. I wanted to come and see you first so that I could digest it in one go.”

An impish smile crossed her face.

"Impatient as always."

He shrugged this remark away and replied.

"I prefer to think it's being efficient on my part."

The Captain blinked as the smile sank away from her face.

"Of course."

The work banter now over, she returned her glance to the flickering computer screen.

"Three days ago. Iroquois Point. 52-year-old female. Single bullet wound to the head. Illegal rounds. Ruled as suicide."

In his mind, he recalled the incident.

"I'm aware."

The Captain could sense his apprehension but continued the necessary report.

"Something new appeared this morning in the same spot. Found by a bicycle rider. Something different."

David sighed.

He knew in his heart that the Captain wouldn't give him a summons on a report without it being urgent, ugly or unsettling.

"Go on."

The Captain continued, reading the information on her computer screen.

"A new body. The body of her son, Michael, who was reported missing ...." she clicked on the mouse a few times.

"Two years and four days ago."

He remembers it despite the fact it was so long ago.

He remembers that the mother would visit the police station every day for months on end. She would show up wearing her work outfit, clung to her body with the day of sweat and effort behind her.

The first fourteen days were spent in condolence and reassurance. He'd be back soon enough; the city takes a toll on all of us."

The police were still looking for him, but it wasn't until after a month that they considered he wasn't going to come back.

His work colleagues were questioned, and even one or two people were suspected; in that line of work, you're going to attract negative attention sometimes.

But no, all the alibis were indisputable and airtight.

The casino CCTV showed him leaving the pit 5 minutes after his shift was due to end. The discrepancy was due to an indecisive or drunk player that caused the delay in his last turn of the cards.

He walked into the dressing rooms of the casino and then, 20 minutes later, clocked out. The last footage of him was walking down an alley towards the strip, mingling with a hundred or more tourists and townsfolk, settling into the night.

He was gone. Up and vanished without a trace.

David could see the Captain pause as he recalled the once-forgotten and closed incident report.

She removed her glasses and made stern and solid eye contact whilst she wrung her fingers together in discomfort.

If her body language was to be believed, it was something very unsettling, very urgent and very ugly.

She spoke in slow and painful tones.

"The body of Michael Young was found bisected this morning by a cyclist. Split clean down the middle. He was found exactly where his mother's body was only days earlier. The forensic team is there now. This is your case, and now it takes priority over all others. The last thing we need is a press field day over this. You should take Detective Williams with you if you think he's ready."

David shook a stern shake of his head.

"Respectfully, no Ma'am. He isn't. He shouldn't see that so early on."

David remembered the first body that he encountered.

It was his third day on the job, he was matched alongside an aged partner, Henry Lloyd. The scene was a road accident. The body was a young Asian woman; barely 19 years old. Her jet-black hair was sprinkled with ebony white skull fragments, all muddied and full of gore. He remembers the smell. It smelled of iron and stale meat. Like an abattoir.

Detective Jacob Williams had been with them just over three weeks now, a fresh-faced recruit who was eager to impress and prove his worth. David knew something like this could ruin him as the job had done to him many years ago.

The Captain nodded solemnly.

"Such a shame."

The tiniest look of resignation crept across her face before she ended the conversation.

"In any case, it's your call Detective. If you need any resources, they are yours, as always."

David could not shake the feeling that he had disappointed the Captain with his decision, but he knew it was the right call to make.

"Thank you, ma'am."

He stood up from the chair using the muscles in his knees, he grunted in complaint at the effort as he made his way back towards the elevator. His thoughts and considerations raced through his mind.

Suicide.

Now, a horrific site of brutality on the same hilltop.

Mother and son.

Reunited in death.

A shudder crept down his core, a reactionary instinct, the definition of a gut feeling.

This won't be the only death.

Not by far.

I promise you this.....

He recalls this phrase to himself as his memory dredged up the familiar smell of Golden Virginia hand-rolled tobacco lit on fire in thin paper wrapping.

Chapter 4: Weaving Spiders Come Not Here

CORNUCOPIA

The Master entered the room.

Throughout the dim space lit only by gaslight, a harrowing screech echoed.

A call of the wild; it is something that should be soaring but now was tethered and tied.

The Master's eyes twitched in eager anticipation; wrapped around their head is a ceremonial mask, the inside of which is carefully covered with crushed velvet around the inlays.

It is a pale and ashen grey visage highlighted with dark royal purple and crimson, painted with intricate weaves that formed holy sigils. They are the ancient symbols of the creator themselves.

Their soft and muffled breath warmed their face as they surveyed the shackled thing before them.

Each day the Master woke; they opened the chest at the foot of their bed. It held the bones of their only heir. They caressed the bare and bleached skull as if brushing hair away from the child's eyes, yet neither were there, just an ebony white dust softly crumbling.

They meditated on this feeling of emptiness.

An all-encompassing and suffocating hollow.

They felt at this moment that the world, the universe and all the intrinsic and essential forces that surrounded them had swallowed them whole in an absolute and complete bleakness. They began to weep guttural, deep and pained tears.

CORNUCOPIA

As they walked along the passageway, they imagined with every footfall that they were entering a thick pool of the very essence and living lifeblood of the universe. It soaked and jostled their body; it brought a tingling hum against their toes.

This was the first step.

They took a heavy leather gauntlet that rested on a table and slipped their left hand into it; their fingers slithered, flexed and writhed inside the holes of the warm, tanned hide.

They moved slowly; their footsteps inched silently but rang aloud with a mind-splintering purpose.

They imagined a thick fog now moving past their knees, entering their genitals. They felt a holy presence living inside them, waiting patiently to be expelled.

Closer and closer still they ambled to the beast that is hooded and strung.

Silent and still.

Upon a five-foot ornate mahogany perch, their talons and legs bound, a regal and magnificent animal stood waiting for the slaughter.

It is a bald eagle, vast and imposing. A heaving, breathing majesty, a symbol of the country in which they lived, representing freedom, liberty and justice for all.

They took a deep breath, steeling themselves.

They imagined that the foggy ether was now covering their torso and head; it released a thousand synaptic explosions in their psyche. Their psychedelic physical, spiritual shell.

Their thought centred upon the endless cosmos, the eternal and infinite sprawling chaos, themselves only a meaningless speck inside of it. They were insignificant, momentary, and invalid.

They ground their teeth in anger and surveyed what was about to happen.

A lightning-fast hand grabbed the eagle's razor-sharp jaw. Its legs flailed; uselessly, it kicked against the knots of rope held around them.

One of its massive wings flapped, suddenly striking the Master's torso. It drew a faint scratch, shedding the tiniest drop of blood.

The realisation of pain brought them back into the moment at hand.

Stinging nerve endings in their core pulsated, sending a shock of feeling, an abrupt end to their descent into the void. An escape from the abyss.

They smiled a vicious grin.

With their free hand, they grabbed the same wing that struck them and pulled viciously.

They felt the tendons and ligaments tear and break beneath the golden-brown feathers. With two solid and hateful pulls, the wing came loose from its body; the eagle's blood covered the sparse brick floor.

The beast screamed the whole time, desperate for escape, despairing for an end to carry them far away from the pain it felt.

The Master granted it this boon.

CORNUCOPIA

Removing its bonds and hood, the Master took a small and petty delight in shoving the torn and tattered being off its perch. It slumped to the ground, writhing helplessly.

The bird, its blood still pouring from its flank, made eye contact with its tormentor. Its irises were a pure orange burning fire, its pupils an endless black chasm.

It is no longer a predator. It is the prey.

A bird of prey.

This thought made the Master chuckle; it was a cruel twist of fate, a hidden contrast all too common in this horrible world.

They pulled a long, curved blade from a scabbard on their side. Silver and etched, the steel sang a shrill hymn as it scraped from its nest.

They lunged and swung directly at the eagle's neck. In one swoop, the scimitar effortlessly decapitated it, cutting through bone and flesh, ending its suffering in a singular flash of offence.

The Master now spoke, their voice distorted by the now bloodied mask upon their face.

"The foundations of the temple are now laid; we give thanks to our creator, the rod and staff, leading us from temptation, delivering us from sin."

The Master plucked a long feather from the severed wing of the now-dead beast in front of them and pressed it against their bloody torso, smudging it with the scarlet fluid of their lifeblood.

"For as we know, long is the way and hard that out of hell leads to light. The first footfall of the journey is awakening our creator from her slumber. For it is written that once the offerings are complete, our Holy Mother, full of grace, will be awoken to cleanse the earth once more."

In the corner of the room, buried in a hole in the wall, was a plinth upon which rested a small plush pillow.

They proceeded towards it, and the blood-marked feather was placed reverently.

"Glory be upon us all. We continue our work, the first step now completed."

Chapter 5: Horkos, The God of Oaths.

David drove in silence; the radio was now firmly turned in the "OFF" position.

CORNUCOPIA

As much as he had fallen in love with his means of transport over the years, the only hitch; the singular fly in the ointment, was the sound system that automatically switched on when the keys turned on the vehicle's electrics. It was an annoyance; it was a persistent one with no logical fix.

Steering slowly past the busy streets and into the horizon of the desert hilltops, he replayed the intel of the report through his cerebrum as he felt the scorching sun of high noon begin to cool as it started its slow descent into the horizon.

Arriving at the scene, he saw a mob. Flashing bulbs of DSLR cameras twinkled and shone, the sound of a dozen shutters clamouring, hoping to snap a picture of what was hidden.

The fucking media.

Someone had leaked it to them, probably the bike rider who discovered it, taking home a wedge of crumpled cash for their troubles.

The press was being held back by police tape held aloft at hip height by small skinny posts; a series of uniformed officers with arms and palms outstretched; they shouted the usual rhetoric: "There's nothing to see here", "Move along", "Go home, people".

The attention of the press was now drawn to him as David exited his car. The crowd knew him well. They knew best to leave him alone, but today, on this occasion, they seemingly forgot themselves.

A million questions were bombarded at him; the light expelled from the tiny LED bulbs was almost blinding to his hungover irises.

He saw the tent that covered the crime scene not far ahead, so he shoved his way through the crowd of clamouring paparazzi, stoic, silent and stern.

He reached the wall of officers; they lifted the tape before he could reveal his badge, waving him through in recognition whilst holding back the multitude of cockroaches flickering their endless snaps to make the next day's headline.

David Garston stood on the outcrop where the body of Naomi Young was found only a few days prior.

Now laid out in front of him was a corpse, bifurcated, sundered, and dichotomised, as if someone had opened a Mackintosh coat. The greying rib cage was the zipper; their blood was the speckled wet raindrops.

Inside the tent that covered the body from the hot desert wind were three forensic officers garnished head to toe in personal protective equipment.

Chemical spill boots, hazmat suits, surgical face masks, and non-porous latex gloves mingled in a huddled mass of activity.

The stench of the body was immediate. As often as David had encountered it, it never got better, and he never got used to it.

He opened a small pot of topical camphor and eucalyptus balm, scooping a generous amount onto his stubby finger as he smeared it under his nose. He felt his sinuses releasing and head clearing, but most importantly, the wretched stink was blocked.

"Reporting in for information, please", he announced as he waved his golden police badge towards the crowd of blue and white fabric.

A small man emerged from the three, having just photographed the splayed remnants of what was once a human being.

He was bunched over with what looked like a slight hunchback, obviously from countless hours spent lingering over a morgue table.

Speaking with a low growl of a voice that did not belong to a man of such a small height, David recognised him immediately.

Kevin Donne was one of the department's leaders in the local PD, Head of blood spatter analysis and Chief of the county coroner's office. David was well aware of his direct and often curt approach. He knew to not take it personally; he was just doing his job. He wanted to distance himself from the horrors of what he saw daily. There is no gallows humour or sly remarks here. Pure business was done cleanly and efficiently.

"David. We're just about done here. Primary reports show the person has been dead for at least 24 hours. Rigor mortis has set in. As you can see, the body is split into two pieces. I've found that this is the result of one singular approach of a long and very sturdy and sharp blade. There are no instances of repeated hacking; this was done in one singular blow. The blood shows me that it has pooled under the corpse pieces themselves, but there was no evidence of any other blood in the surrounding area. We've found pictures on file from what remains of the face on the database. Michael Young. He was drunk and disorderly 6 years ago. He has been missing for quite some time. The body was found this morning by some guy out for a morning spin. You will know by now that his mother was also found here a few days ago. A suicide."

David nodded in acknowledgement.

"Thank you, detective. Any personal effects?"

Kevin touched his hips as if he had already made his points clear.

"Nothing. The subject was found naked."

"Anything else to report or primary considerations?"

The short man replied quickly; he took slight offence to the question he was asked.

"No. I would tell you otherwise."

David tutted to himself and replied with a response designed to be diplomatic, if not slightly passive-aggressive.

"Things are never easy, huh, Kev?"

Kevin responded with a quick shrug of the shoulders as he turned his back to David and continued to snap photos of the scene.

David flipped the bird to his turned back as he exited; he heard the chuckle of approval from the two other investigators inside before they continued to write scribbled notes on small scraps of bound paper.

Sighing quietly to himself, David kicked the dirt on the desert hilltop.

No blood spatters plus dead at least 24 hours equals the body was brought here.

It would have taken great effort to achieve this and a lot of planning. As well as this, it was on the exact spot where the mother was found.

David knew in his heart that the killer, or most likely killers, were highly intelligent, highly motivated and highly skilled. They have resources and patience as their allies.

David tries to imagine the once-living body of Michael and how it could have ended up in two pieces. He couldn't work it out. It didn't compute. Even with motive, the people who did this were full of malice. Dread seeped into his body. This was something very big and very evil.

His eyes swept across the horizon; the heat from the afternoon sun caused a mirage of refraction to wash and wave over his vision; the city appeared to be submersed and sunken in a silver-polished typhoon. High-rise buildings and casinos are trapped in waves.

As he turned to go back to his car, something caught his eye. It was something curious and out of place. A speck of blue was poking out from underneath a red rock nearby.

Curiosity took the better of him as he withdrew a pair of latex gloves from his trouser pocket; he huffed into them before placing them over his paws.

Lifting the rock furtively, slowly, he plucked up in between his fingers what was an empty matchbook. Looking at it through squinted eyelids, he saw beneath the dirt rough handwriting that quickly opened his eyes wide in astonishment. "I'm here. Be back soon. Michael. XxXxX".

Turning the matchbook over in his gloved fingers, he saw the name of a dive bar that haunted the strip.

Vincenzo's Bar & Grill.

He was familiar with it. There were a few arrests for drugs and fights over the years, but it was nothing that was out of the norm. He had once heard rumours about a secret side club, accessed by a code to get in. One of those weird, speak-easy fads. He could see that someone had written the beginnings of a series of numbers; the corner of the matchbook was missing a sizable chunk. Grabbing a plastic evidence envelope, he carefully slid it inside and sealed the zipper.

An alarm beeped on his digital wristwatch, signalling that he was now off duty. He knew he wasn't going home anytime soon. The day was still young. He was going to find answers.

He recalled the sound of a deep, oaken voice that belonged to a person that he once made a solemn oath to. It rang like so:

"I promise you this....."

Chapter 6: Hard Boiled

CORNUCOPIA

The buzzing neon light sounded like a damaged tattoo machine, hammering magnets chattering and colliding with one another.

It radiated a pale coral blue halo that bounced off the soaking wet sidewalk.

Inside a ramshackle bar, a thick haze of cigarette smoke lingered alongside the smell of cheap high-proof booze, sweat and stale cocaine.

The smell of grease from over-cooked red meat would have been there as if the kitchen was open, which nowadays it seldom was.

The place currently held about a dozen people; they were the remnants of an after-after party. Sleep-deprived zombified faces haunted the pool table, bathrooms and bar front, milling around like the countless fruit flies that made this place their home.

It was a day like any other.

Fred, a young kid with a face full of freckles and hair as red as a searing coal fire, was on his 5th week of work here.

Fred was a college graduate, almost at the top of his class in a Bachelor of Fine Arts. When it was time to find a job, he took the first one he could after discovering that his higher education was good to no one who lived and worked here.

Once fresh-faced and full of optimism, this place soon removed it. Fred could set his watch by the regulars who would arrive. Every day, same time, same place, same drink and so on, and so on, etcetera, etcetera, ad infinitum.

It'd been about 10 minutes since he'd last served one of the regulars his fourth drink; the barfly would be ready for his next one soon.

Fred went ahead and opened a bottle of beer and placed it in front of him. A grunt and a slow nod showed acknowledgement, and maybe the faintest "Thanks" hidden in his stupor. He added the drink to the tab and put one on there for himself. A double measure. They wouldn't notice by the end.

It was another washed-out space between late night and early morning, intoxicating the custom until the shift ended, reaching endlessly and repeatedly into the dark hours. They arrived time and time again the next day and the day after that, always thirsty for more, never finding an answer at the bottom of an empty glass.

Over on the far side of the bar was a man, someone he had never seen before. He was on his 4th Boilermaker of the night, his teeth chattering, his tan coat, casual shirt, dark chinos and office shoes were soaked through with rain. His jet-black hair was slicked back, and he occasionally honked a loud sneeze into his elbow cuff. He noticed that he was muttering to himself repeatedly. An intoxicated mantra.

Fred noticed the gun on his side. This wasn't an unusual sight, not at all. It was an all too familiar occurrence. It just meant that he'd have to be more alert than usual. The last thing he needed was another shooting in this place, happening between two drunkards over a stupid misunderstanding.

Off in the distance outside, Fred heard the familiar sound of a series of knocks next door; they pierced through the momentary silence in the gaps of the jukebox music. It stopped after three rhythmic taps, followed by a heavy door opening, before being slammed firmly shut. It was from the "Members Only Club" that was technically attached to the bar but legally and theoretically was not. Fred had never been inside, let alone seen inside.

Besides, it wasn't his scene. Hearing the vague hush-hushed stories, it wasn't the place for gentle souls.

As Fred returned to the bar, the man with slick jet-black hair and a drenched tan coat stood alarmingly close. His eyes fixed in a blank but piercing stare. His breath stank of flat beer and scorched bourbon.

The man pushed his head over the metal bar top and mumbled his words through a booze-addled haze to the scrawny bartender.

Fred stood to attention. This man, quiet yet all too deafening in his intentions stood less than a foot away from him. If the countertop wasn't there, he would have felt more anxious, but for now, he was calm.

The man slurred slowly.

"I'll ask you a question 3 times. Only 3 times."

Fred replied. "Go on. I'm listening."

He knew all too well the false sense of importance and power people felt after a few drinks. It's harmless. He knew he just needed to listen momentarily and get it over with. A calming presence and a kind ear to hear their booze-addled enquiry.

The man now replied in an alarmingly sober tone with strenuous annunciation.

"The number. What is the number?"

Fred paused momentarily.

Tip tapping on the bars till he brought up the bill and passed the person's check to the man before him.

"4 Boilermakers. 2 with house and bourbon. 2 with export and tequila. $60."

Fred saw the person standing close to him blink slowly, wiping a gob of spit from his mouth. His eyes were on fire, and a solid frown swept across his face as his nose crinkled in anger. He looked furious.

"That isn't what I meant. Strike One."

The man on the other side of the bar grabbed him by his collar, pulling him close. Fred could smell cologne, at least a few days old lingering on the man's neck.

Fred began to panic; sweat dripped from his brow. There wasn't any backup. The bouncers had long since clocked off. He was all on his own. The man held his palm wide open, threw his hand back, and swung. It stopped barely inches away from Fred's face.

A soft, playful tap. A quick flick from the man's middle finger and thumb stung his cheek. It implied worse things to come if he didn't comply.

The man twisted Fred's face towards where the knocks outside came from; he squeezed his cheeks softly.

"The number. What is the number?"

This was confidential information and not something that was shared openly. The rumours of things that happened behind those doors were something that could end countless lives, including his own.

"Dude, I can't tell you that. It's members-only."

The man frowned sullenly.

"Wrong answer. Strike Two."

The man now took hold with one hand against Fred's lip piercing, which was hanging low against his mouth, a metal girdle that rested on his gums and incisors. Before Fred had a chance to cry out, the man shut his jaw with his other hand, cradling his skull tightly.

An explosion of force from the stranger's biceps propelled him downwards onto the drenched bar top, which was addled with spit and rye.

Fred's face stopped barely a hair length from the hard steel surface; his expression winced for destruction that didn't arrive. A soft squeak of fear seeped from his gullet.

"Third and last time."

A pristinely polished police badge was stuffed under his eye line, crumpling his nose. Fred heard a metal clink; it was unmistakably the noise of a hammer being pulled back on a revolver, ready to be fired.

David Garston's voice was now full of power and focus.

"Listen, I could drag you around back and put a bullet into the back of your head. This isn't my regular carry. This is unmarked, with no serial number. The most common gun in the entire state. It would never lead back to me. It would take no effort. Just a flick of the switch and....."

CLICK

Fred gasped. An empty chamber. He knew in his soul the next one wasn't.

"I'm going to lift your head back up now. You make one move, and I will take you to the floor, drag you outside and end you. All I have to say is you're a dealer operating from this bar. I spotted you. I tried to arrest you. You tried to run."

Fred knew he shouldn't have done that shit out in the open from the moment he started, but it was the only way to make ends meet or at least the only way he knew how.

"So again, I ask you. What.....is.....the....number?"

Fred gulped, and his jaw was let loose. His finger was slamming furiously against the silent alarm button and had been since question 2.

"3 6 9 12",

David Garston gave a wry smile as if coddling a spoilt toddler.

"There. That wasn't so hard, was it?"

David placed a $100 bill on the counter. He removed the lid off a foul jar full of floating white pearls covered in scum and plucked a pickled egg from it; he consumed it in one bite.

Breath brimming with brine, pith and vinegar, he belched:

"Pleasure's been all mine. Don't worry about the change. Maybe buy yourself a new one of those things...." pointing with a damp, stinking finger towards Fred's lip ring.

David stood to leave the acrid scene just as Armoured Response was arriving. Without thinking, he showed his badge to the person on point and immediately pulled rank.

"David Garston. Here, off duty. The situation has been taken care of. Nothing to worry about. Attempted robbery. Luckily, I was here. Isn't that right....."

David looked towards the visibly shaking bartender and fired off a wink.

Fred nodded compliantly.

The stomping boots that entered Vincenzo's Bar & Grill left as quickly as they came, muttering exhausted shuffles into the cold desert night air.

"I promise you this...."

This is his psalm to himself whenever he works a case like this. He imagines deeply within his mind the agony and despair that the victim felt in their last moments on this earth. It is something he has uttered many times before. When he says it, he recalls the face of his tutor, his mentor. Henry Lloyd. The previous Captain before Terri Cauldwell took over. He was the man who took him under his wing in his first month of the service before retiring, a gold watch firmly placed around his wrist.

He touches the object in his coat pocket.

"I promise you this...."

He remembers Henry's deep-set eyes, a dark and weary mahogany brown.

A plastic evidence bag jostled in his pocket gently, within it a pale coral blue matchbook, empty of matches, the reverse of which had a series of numbers scrawled on it and a chunk torn off.

"I promise you this…."

He remembers Henry's smirk, a wry smile that exuded sheer confidence.

David began his long walk home, preparing to be soaked again by the endless downpour. Even though he was soaked and shivering, he held a smile on his face the whole journey through.

His eternal stanza, his endless repeating sentence, pierced the night air.

"I promise you this……"

Chapter 7: 25 or 6 to 4

CORNUCOPIA

Arched fingers rested on the countertop. Their wrinkled skin and their veins underneath popped with adrenaline.

A dozen eyes leered at the saturnalian scene ahead of them.

The feast, the absolving, the rejection and the scourge are all well and truly on the track to redemption.

The analogue to the outside world is dreaming polychromatic and kaleidoscopic visions as they lay writhing on the sacrificial altar, caressing themselves, pulsating in the throes of carnal pleasure. An intravenous drip full of pearly iridescent liquid was entering their body through a hypodermic needle.

A thousand angels kissed their body, bringing lingering ecstasy into their nerves. A waterfall of dopamine submersed their consciousness; countless goosebumps blemished their ruby-red skin, satiated and plump. The earth and sky were full of a million glowing halos, radiating pure and limitless joy inside of them. Serotonin scattered and swept through their soul, washing them from toe to scalp of any negative emotion. Static electric lines jostled in their limbs, a white noise of constant euphoria.

The onlookers observed as the vessels' eyes opened. The vessel's pupils were as wide and deep as the ocean canyon, dark, bottomless and dewy. Hairs standing erect scattered across their arms, a cosmic orchestra tuning its instrument.

"Such wonders we possess on earth. A small part of the maker's wishes is for us to be here for a speck of existence. Imagine now being with them for eternity. Filling ourselves endlessly with the very definition of manna from heaven. Our vessel is feeling, at this very moment, a mere speck, a minute percentage of what our creator has to offer. Pure and endless joy. Free of the treachery and horrors of this world. But the creator needs sacrifice from each of us and a few who are not our brothers and sisters. The heathens, the unbelievers of this careless momentary existence."

The figure who spoke turned and plucked a straight-edge razor, which was sitting on a decorative pillow upon a lectern at waist height. They passed it calmly to their vessel and whispered instructions into their ear.

“Dear child. I call upon you this day for your complete surrender to Our Holy Mother, full of grace. Give witness by your life. Sacrifice yourself for the salvation of this world. Know I am with you, I am grateful, and I too, will have my own offering. Do not be afraid. For it is only by peeling ourselves open to the wide open space of her creation that she shall welcome us back into her kingdom.”

The vessel's eyes opened wider still; their pulse began to race. Their life suddenly had a purpose. A true goal for once in their miserable subsistence. Tears cascaded down their cheeks, exploding onto the concrete mosaic floor beneath them.

"And thus I have created our seed; it is ready to be sewn into suitable ground. An unwilling receptacle. It is known that the hardiest of our creators' works begin in hostile places. The fig tree grows in arid sand and the cactus in dry clay. And so we now open our collective minds and allow this form to fill the whole of our awareness. In the Mother's name, we give our blessings.'

The crowd at the altar began to hum and buzz with chants. Noises expelled from guttural throats in a prolonged singular warble.

“HAIL…..HAIL……HAIL……HAIL…..”

Driven by this, the vessel began to march with purpose. For mile upon mile, hour upon hour, past the city and past the parks, they walked with nothing but their clothes on their back and the blade, the key to their salvation: silver, solid and sharp.

Ultimately, they arrived in front of their goal.

The actual task was now about to begin. The undressing. The rendering of the flesh.

In the throes of pleasure, they hummed a vibrant song into themselves, raising themselves closer to enlightenment. Their purpose was as clear as crystal.

They began to strip their clothes in front of the house on the suburb's edge. Releasing items piece by piece, every inch of fabric that covered them was released in infantile joy and ultimate exultation until they were as naked as the day they were born. Their clothes were no longer a burden to them; they tossed them aside into the gutter.

The wind sent a cold rush down their back, releasing countless endorphins into their bloodstream. What should have felt icy cold and frigid felt liberating and electrifying; their nipples hardened and pointed. The breeze was a gratification, a sign from above from the holy creator that they were following the correct path. The chemicals running through the vessel's system worked in overdrive, sending flashes of harmony and joy through their veins.

The house in front of them was small and quaint: a single-story spread, a copy-and-paste compartment in the grove. Number 93.

The vessel held a tight grasp of the straight-edge razor and placed the knife's sharp side down against the loose and flabby skin under their armpit. They drew a long, sickening, rigid mark. Blood immediately spurted out from the wound, its warmth counteracting the bitter coldness. A thick wave of everlasting devotion and passionate fervour jolted through their body as they passed the blade forward and further down their arm until it stopped at their wrist. The vessel groaned in ecstasy as they continued, line by line, chunk by chunk, carving away at their fleshy shell. A jigsaw of tissue, ready to be disassembled. Purposefully and laboriously, they began to rend and pull the loosened skin off their muscles. Waves of laughter oscillated within them, piercing the night sky.

The house light in front of them turned on, and noises emerged. The occupant would be here soon, so the vessel began to hurry. They acted quickly now, cutting in a frenzy.

Etching and rending, lacerating and incising. Long ribbons of cuticle dismantled from the human husk were placed on the ground on top of and next to their clothes - a juxtaposition, an art piece, a display of heavenly veneration. An undressing, an exhibition of devotion. Stripped of human possessions, deprived of human flesh, stripping the sins off the very face of this earth, piece by bloody piece.

After a few minutes, the door of the house opened.

Jacob Williams, a member of the City PD, had only just finished his 3rd week on the job and was now made witness. A front-row seat to this showing, this vaudevillian viewing of violence and viscera. A horrific display of hell itself.

The vessel grinned deep and wide; their body now flayed and peeled with cruor and carnage.

Screaming an ardent and doleful dirge, they proclaimed, their eyes fixed on the unwilling.

The receptacle of their message, their seed, and their sacrifice to bring this cruel world to a new beginning.

"Hail Our Mother, Full of Grace. My god is thee.
Blessed art thou amongst women, and blessed is the fruit of thy womb."

Pale blue electric eyes came cascading down from beneath their now open eyelids. The vessel cried in reverence.

"Holy Mother, pray for us sinners, now and at the hour of our death."

They placed the razor against their convulsing throat, pulsating in suppressed pain, overridden with pleasure.

Now screaming into the night sky, they made solid weeping eye contact with Jacob whilst chanting the ancient words:

"AGLON, TETRAGRAMMATON, VAYCHEON, STIMULAMATHON, EROHARES, RETRASAMATHON, CLYORAN, ICION, ESITION, EXISTIEN, ERYONA, ONERA, ERASYN, MOYN, MEFFIAS, SOTER, EMMANUEL, SABAOTH, ADONAI.

I CALL YOU. AMEN."

Their tears ceased. The vessel, now whittled and hacked to the bare bones, began to bid their farewell.

"I'm joining her now. Our Holy Mother, full of grace. And her sacrifice now laid empty and devoid of sin."

The last call scratched through the vessel's voice box, the knife impaling through their windpipe, and virulently, it was swept across to below their ear. A deluge of sanguine haemoglobin fell onto the grass of the daisy-strewn turf.

"Good evening, Detective......"

Their body, now emptied and lifeless, slumped onto the ground; their face showed a toothy argent alabaster smile full of heavenly joy.

Jacob stood still, cemented to the earth as still as the empty shell of human existence before him. His mouth was wide open in shock as tears began to roll past his eyes as if trying to wash away the holy terror he had witnessed. He felt a shotgun blast of dread implode within his core; sickening nausea turned his ashen face green. His hands began to shake a slow quiver; it quickly turned into a fever pitch of agitation. He gagged and wretched as bile passed through his gullet and exited his mouth; it covered his knees and turf beneath him.

A black fog encroached on his field of vision, and the gloom of trauma took him, freeing him temporarily from the scene laid out before him.

Blue and red flashing lights emerged in the distance nearing the scene, and the siren's call echoed.

Chapter 8: Epiales' Dividend

CORNUCOPIA

The moon was strung heavy and high in the night sky; it reflected its pearlescent rays downwards across the city.

David arrived home. Touching a plastic chip card to the pressure plate of the towering apartment block, the heavy door of the building opened. Jangling his keys, he singled out two. One for his mailbox, one for his door. He approached the pigeon holes, some of which were hanging wide open, rusted, pilfered and empty. Finding his own number 284, he plunged the key into the lock in a disorderly fashion, struggling against the booze that was in his system. A leaflet from the local branch of Jehovah's Witnesses, a bank statement and a gas bill were shuffled together into his coat pocket from the small metal door before being closed shut and locked once more.

Pressing the call button on the elevator, a small faded red LED turned on in recognition of activity. Entering the metal coffin, he pressed "2". After a few moments and a short walk down a dusty carpeted hallway, he arrived at his door, unlocked it and entered.

His single-bedroom apartment is barely furnished with minimal trim. A fridge, a shower and a bed were all he needed here, as well as a few small luxuries.

A $10 plastic fan oscillated port and starboard in endless repetitive rhythmic sways shuffled musty air throughout the small space.

A well-stocked bar, kitted with Boston shakers, Hawthorne strainers and soda syphons. The bottles on the shelf were regularly used. Bespoke barrel-aged bourbons, rare oak fermented mescals and a collection of fruit systematically refreshed once a week.

A small grouping of art printings covered one of his walls. It was his pride and joy. It was an assortment of Max Klinger's - A Glove prints. Life-sized recreations of the black, grey and white morbid masterpieces were front and centre on the bare alabaster unpainted wall.

On the left-hand side, Homage; a seaside panorama. A wash of sea foam was crushing against the sand, bringing to the coast what could be carnations, or if you looked one way, they could be skulls. On the left of the picture was a skinny tower with a black flag hoisted high, flapping in the sea breeze.

On the right, Salvage, an old man piloting a tiny schooner vessel into the middle of a turbulent ocean resembling locks of jet black and curled wavy hair. The old man rested precariously on the starboard side, almost plunging himself into the rapids beneath him with a boat hook in hand. The hook was aimed at a single ornate black ladies glove floating in the billowing tide.

In the middle, his favourite one of all: Yearnings. A man was sitting upright, weeping in his bed; his head was held gently in his hands, his knees pressed into his orbital bones. A snuffed-out candle sat on his table, and a single black glove was laid on a blanket beneath his feet. Above and behind the bereft man was a converse scene. It was not his room but a flowing mountain path that led upwards into the sky. At the bottom of the trail, motionless and still, stood a skinny human figure, observing stoically. A thin and feeble lemon tree sprouted round and perfect fruits. To him, it was a portrait of hushed yet ear-shattering purpose. A mirror held up to humanity to show its fragility, its removal and yet constant connection to nature and emotion itself.

In a dark room to the side of the small apartment lay his single bed; the mattress and sheets lay crumpled in a pile; it had not been washed in weeks. Next to it, upon a small and functional table, sat a corded telephone and answering machine; its tiny LED was blinking red flashes intermittently. David knew what this meant. It worked. No one else other than scam artists and work ever used his number.

A huff of exasperation exited his mouth; it stank of booze and sulphur. A message at this time was never good. It usually stood as a beacon of emergency or a call to action. He was too drunk, too tired, and yet his curiosity called to him, coaxing him to conclusively press the rewind button. Spluttering into effect, a zigzag of black tape shot across the machine, whizzing garbled noises through the tiny speaker.

A little robotic voice announced:

"YOU HAVE REACHED THE NUMBER OF......."

His voice called in response, "David Garston."

"AT THE SOUND OF THE BEEP, PLEASE LEAVE YOUR NAME, NUMBER AND MESSAGE."

CHIRP....

Crackled static of white noise slowly and softly weaved its way through the empty apartment air. For second after second, there was nothing except this and a stony silence. Then, after a short while, an almost imperceptible sound; the receiver of the calling phone shuffled shakily.

A soft, whispered voice. It was deep, cavernous and profound, full of animosity, authority and power. It had an artificial and mechanical quality to it; the voice was muffled and held restraint.

"Beneath your compassion, we take refuge.
Oh, Holy Mother, full of grace; do not despise our petitions in time of trouble, but rescue us from dangers only pure and blessed ones. Today is the crowning of our salvation and the

manifestation of the Mystery which is from eternity itself; the Son of God becometh the Son of the Virgin, and Gabriel announced the glad tidings of grace, wherefore they let us cry out with him to the Mother of God; Hail, full of grace, you are with thee."

A group of voices sang in unison in a sound that could never be described as harmonic. It sounded like a thousand buzzing flies caught in a thin glass jar. It swarmed and flew; it soared high and rumbled low.

"HAIL..... HAIL...... HAIL..... HAIL......"

"Who will dare to doubt that she who was purer than the angels and at all times perfection was at any moment, even for the briefest instant, not free from every stain of sin?"

A low murmuring groan of compliance responded, all before being returned into the storm of the chant of:

"HAIL......HAIL...... HAIL...... HAIL......"

"Hail our Holy Mother, full of grace, that the encroaching flood shall wash the world clean and free of sin. When Noah warned the unbelievers, they were stuck drowning and sunken. Hail our Holy Mother, full of grace, in which the saints are shaped and formed to give us the power and strength to crush the head of the serpent, overcoming our enemies and for the greater glory we hail."

"HAIL...... HAIL...... HAIL...... HAIL......"

The voice changed direction; it was now focused not on the crowd but on the listening machinery.

"David. We know you. We see you. We ARE you. We know you stand for the same principles as us. Liberty and justice for all. We know you have seen pain. You have seen the world and know it needs to be reborn. We give you this chance. Stand aside. Let us continue our work. Let us complete our will. Perhaps you will be welcome in the arms of the rapture awaiting us. If not, you will become a shredded part of our work, empty, devoid and dead. Choose wisely."

The voice changed intent once more.

"Such wonders we possess on earth...."

BEEEEEP.

NEXT MESSAGE.

The sound of Jacob Williams echoed down the phone line. It was the sound of him deep in despair; he left this message from somewhere buried in the depths of his core, his heavy throbbing breaths racing at a million miles per hour.

"David.....D..dd.Dd David you n. nN Need to listen. They've, they've, they're, they come to me. i I it's.. it's all linked to The Young's. The th. t. Th. Th at was only the start. He. h He s..ss.skinned himself whilst I w w Watched. M m mMy God... I it can't be h h happening."

And then a soft clunk, followed by:

BEEEEEP.

NEXT MESSAGE.

The voice of Kevin Donne entered the room.

It was an unwelcome combination of superiority and braggadociousness.

"David. There's a body that has just arrived now. Make it your priority to come and view it at your earliest convenience.

The word "convenience" made David's teeth clench in anger. His job was never in the least bit convenient.

BEEEEEP.

NEXT MESSAGE.

A soft and gentle female voice emerged; it held a shallow twang of a trained and restrained Southern sand belt accent.

"David. It's Terri. Listen, you're out, and you're off duty, and you might not even hear this, but I need to try anyway."

A deep and long, sorrowful sigh echoed.

"Something happened to Detective Williams tonight whilst he was at home. Such a shame. He was targeted by who we now believe was the next victim relating to the Naomi and Michael Young case. They committed suicide in front of him. Jacob is physically fine; he is not injured in any way. He will, of course, be going through therapy, which I will personally initiate."

There was a solemn pause as the Captain chose her following words wisely.

"You need to listen. When you get home, lock your door and chain it shut. Do whatever you need to do, but do not answer it for anyone until you leave for work. Report anything directly to me immediately. And David....... Please, please stay safe. I don't need to lose you. Take care."

BEEEEEP.

END OF MESSAGES.

David's head swam. It was a mixture of rage, denial and alcohol. What he wanted but did not need was a stiff drink. He ambled over to the bar top and clumsily dragged an ornate low-ball whisky glass out. He opened the miniature freezer and plucked from it a perfect spheroid ice ball that was flawless and clear; he tossed it into the glass with abandon. Squeaking open a bottle of brandy, he poured until the glass almost overflowed.

David's hand covered the top of the icy glass full of brown spiced spirit as he ambled to the front door before locking it firmly. The top lock coughed into place, quickly followed by a second gratifying clunk. He chained the door shut and swung a tertiary fastening device across that slotted and sprung solid into place.

He took a congratulatory pull from his drink and immediately coughed a reactionary splutter; he almost dropped the glass entirely, but he held fast and strong.

He sat down on his battered armchair and flicked a reel-to-reel tape player into life.

Scratchy music played gently; it was a warming blanket of brass horns and percussive piano fills that emanated the room; it momentarily cleared his battered and bruised mind.

He took another drink; this time, he was acquainted with it and did not splutter, yet he winced almost in pain at the taste of hot yet icy cold herbal medicinal ethanol raining across his taste buds.

Without a shower or shave, he closed his eyes and sank into the world of sleep. Tomorrow will be a long day.

He remembers the smell of Henry Lloyd's apartment when he was invited over for drinks. It was leathery and full of dust. Full of booze and sorrow.

"I promise you this……."

Chapter 9: The Defile Of The Axe

The Master entered.

CORNUCOPIA

It is a damp and stench-ridden barn that once would have held a throng of activity, a cornucopia of life thriving in care and comfort. Enclosed beasts, although they were, they grazed green and joyous. But now only one remained, tortured alone and cold. Its broad flank was covered by healed scars and scratches; needles poked through its thick brown hide; it resembled a colossal, lingering, furious porcupine. The dimly lit hut was bathed in a sickly sweet smell, a cocktail of decay and desperation. Blood splatters covered almost every inch of the enclosure; it is a macabre painting of violence and horror.

The Master approached. Memories of their boy once full of life clung to their synapses.

Precious thoughts, moments and memories lodged themselves in their mind; primal urges of protection brought them nearer to what was necessary: the task at hand.

A young boy. Harmless to this world, he was precocious yet solitary; a seedling that had barely sprouted had been severed and removed from this world. They remembered the day he was born. A perfectly formed amalgamation, a pure and complete union between two people that had brought a new life into being. With furrowed brow and a mouth leaking amniotic fluid, they remember his first sound. At the time, it was a mixture of relief and elation; the high-pitched squeals of a newborn travelled through the natal ward. Dark brown hair waved across the cherubim's pristine scalp; they remember how complete they felt. How full and brimming they were with joyous purpose.

The Master remembers the anniversary of his arrival. Blue balloons and ribbons stretched across the ceiling of the gift-filled room. Barely a toddler, the kid had been spoiled rotten on this day. A miniature petting zoo, peanut butter and jelly sandwiches, the latest trendy toy that was enough to bring envy to the other kids on the block.

The memory quickly faded as teardrops from the Master's eyes pitter-pattered on the barn's ground against the rotten hay and soil.

The giant animal was panting heavily; its jet-black eyes were soaking wet and full of fear. The air escaping from the beast's nostrils appeared like steam from a tea kettle; the brute grunted and brayed heavily against its enclosure. Trapped in tight like anchovies in a can, it had no chance of escape.

The Master held in their hand a cordless power drill; its exterior was deeply speckled with asphalt and paint chips. Planted in the chuck was a drill bit, a vicious-looking circle of black metal, its teeth as sharp as a crown of thorns. In their other hand was a long, sturdy chain that trailed behind them like a serpent. On each end were locking hooks, solid and unyielding.

A quick and deliberate button press brought a rotation of activity to the drill; three dozen toughened barbs of hatred whirled into the thick night air. The high-pitched squeal was matched in kind by a low and deep guttural howl from the animal encased in its steel-barred prison.

The Master felt the bull's fear as they walked up to the cage; they carefully placed their skinny hand on the scarred hide near its neck. They felt the echoing pounding pulse underneath the thick leather; it raced and ran wild with fear. It is a bodily drumbeat that is frenetic and dire.

The Master unlocked the hook on the end of the chain whilst caressing the livid and rageful beast, trying to coax it into submission. It huffed in protest as its hoofs kicked up dust in the enclosed trap.

CORNUCOPIA

The hook on the end of the chain clamped across the vast and cold septum, piercing across the wet nostril of the bovine, clicking into place. A ferocious snort of exertion blasted in defence, matched with an equally brutal shove downwards to the ground.

The Master quickly pulled the chain into a locking pinion gear and began to ratchet the metal links downwards to the muck-ridden earth. With each diabolical heave, the bull released gut-wrenching cries of agony. After a few clicks, the gear was sealed and stuck in place. The beast was helplessly glued to the ground. The second offering was now completely unable to move. The Master licked their lips beneath their already blood-speckled mask and lined up their first drill incision into the bovine skull.

A thousand cries of despair roared like a freight train, a caterwauling hybrid of agitation and butchery. The Master carefully, repeatedly and with great care ground hole after hole at the base of the beings left horn where it met the skull, working slowly and laboriously to not enter the brain; their objective was clear.

Distil the very meaning of suffering.
Make it wish it was dead.
And then, at its lowest point, permit it its desire.
Release it back into the void.
Back to the beginning of life.
A fresh start, granting it mercy into the new paradise soon to come.
Shortly, this would occur.
The thought cemented their intent further.

The drill encapsulated fury with every single scorching, smoking incision. It glowed red hot with the effort of pushing against and through broad and thick bone. The smell of burning flesh and animal hair diffused into the air, a stench as strong as titanium.

The Master's gag reflex was barely controlled; their triceps flexed and ached with endeavour; they were sore and cramped. After precisely ten heinous grinds, the Master paused. Proceeding now with care, The Master licked their skinny finger covered in what was once a pearly white leather glove; it had been muddied and speckled in a million ruby red flecks. With a moistened finger, they lay it on the first hole incised, precisely on top.

"Kether. The Crown."

And so they continued, repeating the invocation for each bloody incision.

"Binah. Chochma. Geburah. Chesed. Tiphereth. Mod. Netzah. Jesod. Malchuth."

In front of them, the bull was on the precipice of its death; it now lay vacant and worthless, its life quickly fading. Seeing this, they acted quickly. Rapaciously, The Master usurped a hold of the loosened horn that was barely holding on, limply hanging by remnants of cartilage and ossein. With a hard pull powered by their biceps, it came loose.

"A seizing and giving. The fire of the living. Tis thus at the roaring loom of time I ply and weave for our creator the garment thou seest her by."

With a hole now revealed, The Master saw a veiny and soaking red organ barely hidden by a mosaic of ivory-white calcium. The brain beneath seemed to pulse, its synapses sending the last series of pain receptacles into the flaccid giant, now helpless on the ground.

The Master held the bloodied horn triumphantly and spoke in thunderous tones muffled by the fabric covering their mouth.

"And thus the second offering comes to being. Our mother will send on you curses, confusion and rebuke on everything you put your hand to until you are destroyed and come to sudden ruin because of the evil you have done in forsaking her. Our mother will plague you with diseases until she has destroyed you from the land. Our mother will strike you with wasting disease, with fever and inflammation, with scorching heat and drought, with blight and mildew, which will plague you until you perish. Our mother's curse is on the house of the wicked, but she blesses the home of the righteous."

They inverted the sharp end of the horn downwards, high above their head, as they felt the creator's power strike through the muscles of their grasped and solid fist. A swift plunge into the brain of the beast released a blood-ridden splash; it matched the already dried coagulation on The Master's dirty ornate mask.

The bull released its final sigh, a death rattle from deep within itself. The Master's job was complete; they withdrew the horn from the cattle head and reopened the wound on their torso with the sharp point of the funnel of rock-solid keratin.

They felt the tip of the sharp tusk penetrate them. A blood offering, one animal, one human. They passed the eagle's feather and found another alcove sunk into the wall, which stood a plinth with a simple velveteen cushion. They lay the soaking wet horn, still dripping with cortex and plasma, upon the soft velour surface.

"Glory be upon us all. We continue our work, the second step completed."

Chapter 10: Lady Wisdom

Terri Cauldwell, the Captain of the PD, is the assigned therapist for today's session. She could have chosen someone else to lead, but no, she owed it to Jacob to take care of this personally, at least at the preliminary stage. Terri adjusted her glasses and opened the door into the soft wooden room. She looked at her patient, her officer, her friend.

His name is Jacob Williams; his head was buried within his hands, and his body shook and jittered as he paced up and down the room, never stopping to breathe, not for a single moment. She knows what happened to him but asks him nevertheless. An attempt at breaking the current mental block happening to him.

“You need to tell me what happened, Jake. You need to slow down, calm yourself and talk to me.”

Jake remained silent and distraught, a human locomotive of despair caught within emotional handcuffs. Most people's immediate response to life-changing events is one of four responses.

Fight, flight, fawn or freeze.

Typically, narcissists tend towards fight; they are controlling people with anger issues. There was no shred of rage within Jacob's body.

To freeze is reserved for people who struggle to make decisions; they are often emotionally numb and tend to dissociate. Another no.

Fawning is reserved for people-pleasers, co-dependent, identity-confused and without boundaries. No.

Flight was the only option left. People who tend to ruminate, obsess and perfectionist workaholics. This was Jacob to a tee.

He started at the department three weeks ago and since then has been at the pinnacle of professionalism. His outfit was pressed and starched to an army standard. His hair was cut every two weeks to the same regulatory measures. His brunette hair was cropped down to almost nothing, a flat uniform perfection that was designed to instil respect and trust.

An army kid since birth, his dad perpetually moved from site to site, from state to state. Sergeant Bryan Williams was awarded a Purple Heart for his time during Desert Storm. His father, his idol, his mentor, was cut down all too soon by the scum of humanity. His father put his life on the line for the principles of this country; he was one of the fallen but never forgotten.

Jacob was only 16 when his father was killed. Bryan Williams, a hero of war, was cut down in his prime by a fucking carjacker in broad daylight. A junkie, a reprobate, a dark stain on the blue-collar of this world. Itching for a score, he chose Bryan Williams' car while still at a stop light. As his Father scrolled the window of his sedan to pass the man the change from his pocket, a knife quickly entered through the window and slashed his throat from ear to ear. A vicious, unprovoked attack that haunted Jacob for years to come.

He was never given the chance to view the body before the burial. His mother forbade it. She was protecting him, saving him from more misery. Jacob did not see it this way; he thought he was being coddled and controlled unnecessarily. He never fully forgave his mother for it. Every conversation after the tragedy was a cruel reminder of a life well lived that was taken away far too soon.

At his Father's funeral, he didn't cry. Not even during the gun salute, not even when the wreath and perfectly folded flag were placed upon the solid oaken coffin, did Jacob shed a tear. He felt utmost pride and joy that his father had acted with poise, grace and heroism in the face of adversity. Jake was proud, not sorrowful. He wished that everyone put on this earth could be this pious, this valiant as to lay down their lives for what is real and right, for justice.

Jacob had to be steely and unshaken, yet what he had been made witness to last night cut him to his core, to his raw and unhealed wound of trauma. The noise of it was what hurt the most. The sound of the sharp knife piercing the man's throat; Jacob could not help but imagine that it would have sounded the same as his father's death. A deluge of blood squirted across the earth, draining and seeping across the shoe and sole.

“JAKE”

For this single syllable, the only occurrence of the voice that emerged from the Captain's mouth was his Fathers. A solid oaken timbre, a deep drone from the depths which rattled his eardrums and split his soul. He was forced to a halt. Jake looked at the Captain's lips in disbelief, noticing the slightly wrinkled crow legs beginning to grace her stern yet caring face.

“JAKE”

It was the Captain's voice this time. A Southern drawl tamed by time, tide and practice. A smooth and silken tone, full of guardianing protection. Jake dropped to his knees and began to sob for one of the first times since he was a kid. He wept thick, dense and burdenful tears of agony. Jake screamed into the void; an eternal howling wail deafened any noise that may have been present. He felt the darkness edge around his vision, a creeping miasma ready to take over him. A black and thundering mist crackled with white bolts of fury; he began to see stars, a kaleidoscope of blood vessels bursting inside his mind.

“JAKE. I NEED YOU BREATHE, OK?"

Lines of purple, red and white danced in front of him, a glimmer within the dark that now almost completely enveloped him. His head swam like three sheets in the wind; the last remnants of oxygen within his cells were now being depleted by his heart that still churned, ever restless.

A quick and sharp exhale was immediately followed by a gasp of air inwards repeatedly, a sonorous stampede propelling and gasping for breath. A cavalcade of quick bursts, desperate and brutish, clinging uselessly to the edges of sentience.

"   Jake........."

"   jake........"

Slumping knees to the floor, he flopped over face forwards and merged atoms with the carpet below him. To him, it felt as if he was sinking beneath the floorboards, entering a new dimension. A reality similar and adjacent to dreaming, but something darker and more desperate.

He lay sprawled on the floor with his limbs contorted at unnatural angles. A thin film of sweat coated his pallid skin, causing his features to glisten with a sickly, otherworldly sheen. A tangle of matted hair veiled his face, leaving only glimpses of the twisted expression beneath. The slow, laboured rise and fall of his chest was the sole indicator that life still clung to his fragile form.

Within the confines of his unconscious mind, a macabre creation, a spectacle unfolded inside himself. His mind's eye conjured grotesque figures that slithered and skulked through the murky recesses of his thoughts. Shadows took on sinister shapes, looming over their hapless prisoner. Twisted, distorted versions of his Mother and Father whispered malevolent secrets, their voices and words dripping with venomous intent.

"You were never good enough."

"Do you think you could ever be my equal?"

"Look at yourself, crawling and caterwauling in the muck. You disgust me."

The visions of his past mistakes materialised into twisted and grotesque monstrosities, their eyes as wide as television screens, they projected back to himself a gruesome parody of his failures. The cacophony of internal voices grew louder and louder, a chorus choir of anguish reverberating within his cortex.

As time stretched on, his internal struggle became more palpable. His unconscious form twitched sporadically, the torment of his trapped psyche manifesting physically. His fingers clenched and unclenched in a futile attempt to escape the nightmarish realm he found himself in. His lips trembled as if trying to voice a plea for release from the horrors he faced within his mind.

In this grim tableau, the line between reality and imagination blurred. The realm of Jake's unconscious mind had become a sinister prison, its walls closing in with every passing second. Jake's body twitched and shook on the warm carpeted floor; he was a mere vessel for the unspeakable battle taking place within his tortured psyche.

Terri lifted his head in her hands and shook his body to rouse Jacob from his nightmare.

"JACOB. WAKE UP. YOU NEED TO SPEAK TO ME."

Softly, his breathing returned, now at a slow pace. His head lay in the lap of his Captain, his confidante; his tears still streamed from his eyes.

“Its…..its…I’m okay… I’m okay.”

Terri responded quickly.

“No, Jake, you’re not.”

Jake nodded as he scrubbed his eyes with the sleeve of his shirt.

"No, Ma'am, I don't suppose I am."

Terri calmly brushed her hand through Jacob's wiry hair lovingly.

"You know Jake, I knew your Father. He was a great man. You may not remember, but I was the officer on the scene that day. That awful day. I promised your mother that I would be there for you. Always watching. There's a reason why I fought so hard for you to be in our department. Because I know you are special. I know you are strong. I know you can recover from this and see it through to its right end. Never, ever think you're weaker for feeling these things. It shows you're ready for change, ready to fight for what is correct."

"Ma'am. I just can't comprehend why. I can't understand it. He…"

Jacob almost vomited at the memory of seeing the man's flesh rip from the muscle. He remembers seeing the tendons twitching, fighting against the pain, but the man was not searching for recourse. He seemed almost elated in the agony.

"He tore the skin off his body. And then…"

Another heave; this time, he produced a flow of sickly yellow bile from the depths of his stomach. He remembered the blade of the razor entering the man's throat, the last gurgle of air escaping from his lungs. The final twitch from the tormented corpse flinched before his eternal, everlasting rest.

"I know Jake. The same death as your Father."

Jacob stopped crying. He rolled over and punched the floor suddenly. A faint thump thudded against the carpet, releasing a tiny puff of ancient dust from the fibres.

"HE FUCKING KNEW. HE KNEW ABOUT MY DAD. HE KNEW HOW HE WAS KILLED. AND HE FUCKING TORMENTED ME WITH IT."

"Jacob. Come on. You know that's not possible. It's a cruel coincidence. Yes, he knew you were police. As disgusting as it is, people despise us. Even though we are there for their protection. We are siblings in a society that believes it is an only child. A spoiled child at that. But that is our burden. That is our task. We are the thin blue line."

Jacob looked up at her and peered into her caring eyes. She had shed tears; her muted mascara had started to run down her pale cheek.

"Ma'am, respectfully, I need to take some time. I need to straighten myself out. To figure out where to take this. I want to work with Detective Garston. I believe that this is intrinsically linked to him and to the case that he is working."

Terri smiled a troubled smile.

"Jacob. I will always support you. I will always do what is best. If you believe this is what you should do, you have my everlasting support. BUT. I advise against this. David, as valued as he is, can be intense. You know this."

Jacob slowly nodded.

"The last thing you need is another shock. Take your time. Come back to us when you're ready."

Jacob stood, dusted himself off, straightened his tie and swept his messed wiry brown hair to the side.

"Thank you, ma'am. As always"

Terri Cauldwell remained sitting on the floor where she was as she watched the young detective leave through the heavy wooden door.

She knew in her heart of hearts that Jacob would do what he wanted.

Such a shame.

Huffing to herself lightly, she stood and wandered to the door and exited, locking it behind her.

Jacob would never be the same, and she knew it.

Such a shame.

Chapter 11: Backstage Pass

David woke from his slumber still nestled in his armchair. His head and stomach groaned in protest.

His body was losing a one-sided fight against a vicious hang-over. Creamy white flaking froth clung to the sides of his lips, a collection of crust gathered in the recesses of his eyes, thorny and stiff.

Steeling himself, he propelled himself to his feet quicker than his body was ready. The alcohol still swimming in his system fought against him; a solid wave of tipsiness forced him back to being prone on the chair. He looked over his shoulder, causing a tidal force of nausea to fly across him. Barely holding on, squinting, he saw his alarm clock. It read “07:05” in a faint and flickering shade of blue. He still had time. Fleeting as it was, he still had time.

The desert sun shone heavy and steadfast, creeping through the shuttered plastic roller blinds. He huffed and smelt his sickening, stale breath. In disgust, he pressed firmly on the armrests with fists like vice grips. He forced his legs upwards slowly and full of care. Steady this time, he stumbled towards the shower, removed his clothes and proceeded to scrub the sweat and muck from his body. His plain clothed uniform was hung in the corner of the room; he hoped the steam from the hot water would ease the creases on his pale blue collared shirt.

Finishing his ablutions, he exited the stream; he dried himself off quickly, leaving his hair damp and messy. He applied speed stick deodorant and clothed himself. He sprayed a quick blast of aftershave on his cheeks even though his face was full of stubble.

Memories of the previous night's phone messages replayed across his mind. He pressed PLAY on the machine as he slipped on his shoes and began to tie the knot. It was real, then. Not a nightmare. Not a false memory. His thoughts stopped on Jake. He hoped he was alright but knew deep down that he would never be the same again.

Time to move. He had things to do before starting his shift at Noon. First, coffee. Second, food.

David walked to a window and, with two fingers, peered through the closed plastic, barely keeping the morning sun from entering. A bright sun flare blinded him temporarily; his pupils dilated in protest. Today will be a sunny one. The skies emptied themselves of their tears last night.

CORNUCOPIA

He clipped his shiny golden badge to his hip and attached his gun holster to his back. He slipped his standard-issue pistol into it; it was loaded and full of death. It was heavy and uncomfortable, but after all these years, he couldn't imagine walking and living without them.

He unlocked his front door and headed out, not before locking and bolting it from the outside. Meandering down the hallway, he reached the elevator and pressed the CALL button. After a few moments longer than usual, David looked up at the lift door and noticed a sign. "OUT OF ORDER", it read in a hurried, scrawled and careless text. He tutted to himself and started to traipse down the stairs.

Reaching the front lobby, he could now start to hear the hum of the city. It was a noise that never stopped. It consisted of footsteps, excited voices and cellular phone chimes; it was like being trapped inside a busy restaurant full of idle chatter and clinking forks for all eternity.

He reached outside and headed to his usual spot. It is a 24-hour diner just a few short doors from his apartment block. Swinging the door open, he took a seat at the nearest table. He didn't need to see the menu. He had the whole thing memorised with the amount of times he visited. Gary will be working today.

After a few short moments, a tall man with skinny fingers in his mid-20s approached. He wore the uniform. A white short-sleeved shirt with yellow and pink stripes. An apron with four pens in its front pocket that was adorned with badges saying things like "Always happy to help", "Service with a smile", and "Hi! My Name Is....GARY...."

"Hey, David. I don't suppose I need to ask what you're having?"

The youngster spoke; his voice still sounded like it was barely breaking through puberty.

"Ever so predictable, Gary?"

David rolled his eyes in slight embarrassment.

"Yep. Send it on its way."

David plonked $30 into the server's hand, which was the total of his order plus a generous tip on top.

He began to drift into a slumber in the plastic-coated cushioned seats but was awoken shortly after by the smell of coffee and cut meats approaching his table. A triple shot of coffee with a dash of cream and cold water to the top in a large takeaway cup. A bacon, salt beef and American cheese submarine roll topped with two runny eggs almost to the point of being raw permeated under his nostrils; it was all wrapped up in grease-soaked paper and chopped in two.

He quickly sank half of the tepid brown liquid into his throat and devoured half of the sandwich in three enormous bites. Barely suppressing a belch, he felt waves of relief washing over him; this was his perfect cure for the regularly occurring katzenjammers.

Picking up the remnant, he wandered out the front door, muttering between full and crumbled yolk-soaked lip, something that sounded like "Thank you".

His head was still fuzzy, but his aim was precise.

He rambled down the strip, passing theatres, strip clubs, casinos, restaurants and bars, all with his mission fixed in his mind. After twenty minutes of walking, he had finished his breakfast as he arrived outside police headquarters.

Ambling straight through the revolving front doors, he waved his badge to the receptionist, who nodded a quick acknowledging reply. The silver archway of the metal detector furiously chirped an alarm as he passed through. A crowd of eyes looked up at him in inquiry as he produced a slim plastic card on his key fob to a detector on the elevator door. It opened after a few moments with a cheerful chime. Entering, he pressed the button "5".

A few moments passed before the doors opened once more. The bullpen revealed itself to David; it was empty and bare. Not a soul in sight, just the vacant hum of computers on idle; the water dispenser belched a single trickling bubble.

He could hear a crowd, though. The noise was coming from the conference room. Marching down the hall, he ventured closer, and it became louder and louder still. A cacophony of a million questions battered the space ahead of him, a solid mechanical "CLICK CLICK CLICK" of camera shutters activating. He could see now that the Captain was standing in front of a pedestal in a room packed to the brim with both seated and standing news reporters. David saw her; she stood as stiff as a board; her tie was knotted tightly around her neck, and a single bead of sweat started to roll down her cheek. This was the only Achilles Heel that David knew that the Captain had.

Crowds.

Watching on the outside of the room was Andrew Liston. A CSI, he was one of the crew and one of the team. Andrew had been with this station for 4 years since moving away from his previous assignment on the other side of the country. Whispers spoke that he had gone through a particularly unpleasant divorce. When questioned about this, Andrew refused to speak of it, so the rumours and chattering spread like wildfire. Although he dressed poorly and spoke with an accent that didn't belong, he fit in with the squad with minimal fuss; he was a professional through and through. David and Andrew had met on his first assignment with the station: a homicide relating to a turf war between two dealers; it was another daily occurrence in the city basin, nothing out of the ordinary. They shared drinks after almost every case they worked, talking until the early hours about how wrong the world was and how rotten it was at the core. Only once did he mention his wife after too many shots of tequila. The separation resulted from too much time spent on the job and not enough with her. It is the old and cliche tale of a devoted cop involved too much with work, caring too little about those closest to them.

He nodded to Andrew, and he replied in kind. There was no need for pleasantries here.

"Boss hates this," Andrew muttered partly to himself. "A media circus.".

David shook his head, deep in disapproval at the vultures in the room, barraging, bellowing and hungry.

A squawking voice rang from the back of the conference room, a tape recorder lifted above the heads of the bustling mess of the crowd.

"Captain, is it true that this latest victim was found outside one of your own officer's residences?"

The Captain blinked sternly and gave an angry retort.

"I refuse to answer any questions relating even closely to the personal nature of these proceedings. If another question like that is asked, you will be left with an empty stage."

She shook her head in admonishment at the reporter, making sure to make her feelings clear to him.

"Such a shame."

It was as if she was reprimanding a spoiled brattish child for speaking out of line.

"NEXT."

The Captain shook her head in disgust and made eye contact with David. Her eyes, a usual shade of blue, now seemed on fire. He could see the blood vessels in the whites, her veins popping in stress.

"Captain, what exactly CAN you tell us about this?"

"What I CAN tell you, SIR, is that I dislike your tone. Rest assured, you ladies and gentlemen, that we have our best officers on this case, working tirelessly to bring this series of crimes to a stop."

The room went silent for a split second. A heavy mistake has just been made.

"What exactly do you mean SERIES of crimes? Has this happened before? Is it in connection to something else? What is it you're hiding, CAPTAIN?"

Terri Cauldwell buried her head in her hands before exiting, muttering a sharp "Interview over" into the microphones.

A typhoon of camera flashes, a chorus of unanswered queries, the press was held back from her by armed officers at her side who escorted her out of the room and away, as far away as they could manage.

Mopping her brow and replacing her jacket, she approached David. She looked as white as a sheet.

"David......"

"Yes, Ma'am?"

"End this."

"Yes, Ma'am."

She left with urgent immediacy as she entered her office before locking the door and closing the thin, steely blinds that covered her window.

Andrew muttered an apologetic "Best do what you're told David....." before walking off solemnly towards his desk.

David paced towards the elevator once more and pressed the button "B2". The Morgue.

After a short descent, the doors opened to a long and steely hallway, at the end of which sat a heavy metal door and a kiosk in which a receptionist was clicking away idle-mindedly on the keyboard of a desktop computer.

He spoke loudly and intently to the person behind the solid plastic barricade.

"Officer reporting. David Garston. Badge 5278."

The young man looked up and made eye contact with him. He tip-tapped a few buttons, and after a few seconds, he produced a clipboard with a sheaf of dog-eared papers attached. On it were rows and columns of lines, each filled with signatures, time in, time out and the coroner on duty.

"Sign in, please."

David scrawled his signature as he checked his watch and etched "08:10". Surveying the board behind the wall, he saw the writing "Coroner on duty - Waylon". The name was written in a beautiful embellished italic script.

David sighed a breath of relief. He wouldn't have to deal with Kevin.

The day was starting to turn in his favour, if only slightly.

He was buzzed in, and the solid door clunked open loudly. Beyond was a vast room, perfectly sterile and frigid. Erlenmeyer flasks were filled with odd-coloured liquids, and refrigerators hummed idly to themselves. In the centre was a metal table upon which was a vaguely human shape covered in a black tarpaulin material. Next to it sat Patricia Waylon; she was one of the coroners under the wing of Dr. Kevin Donne's domain of death. Her curled brunette hair was barely restrained by a surgical cap, and her mouth was covered with a thin paper mask; this only enhanced and illuminated her already bright blue sapphire-coloured eyes. She turns and notices the officer in the room and begins to speak in an accent with the slightest incline of Italian descent.

"Hello, David. I'm just about to finish up. I'll tell you one thing: I've never seen anything like this. It's a bad one, a real bad one. Just a heads up."

Her tanned skin seemed to turn pale at the memory.

"I've heard. Captain left a message with me, as did Jake."

Although David couldn't see her mouth, he could tell by her eye language that she was wincing away a repellent thought.

“Show or tell?” the coroner asked.

David sighed in resignation.

“Let’s get it over with.”

The hand of the coroner reached across and held the slippery black fabric between her fingers before slowly removing it like an overripe banana peel.

David thought he was prepared; he believed he had mentally steeled himself for the worst.

He was not ready.

The shape of the being beneath the sheet was a human being that was torn and stripped apart. David had seen the meat of muscle before; red, sanguine and exposed, he had seen the bare blankness of bone, but not like this.

The being's hair was intensely black and matted solid with rocky pebbles of scabbed blood. An eyeball crept out of its socket; it has no eyelid to keep it in its place. Where there should have been lips, there was only a yellowing white display of teeth; any remnant of the mouth covering was shredded and misplaced. The corners of the mouth were upturned in a stretched grin; they were forever more in a state of elation. Excoriated, violated and abraded, the body was a poor imitation of a life once lived, a soul once filled. David could see the very fibres of the muscle, the tangled mess of red veins and nerve endings now lying still and at rest.

The throat was perhaps the worst part. It was a feral and brutal force that had carved a sudden cylindrical cave-in of skin, flesh, and tissue to be torn away, an empty hollow that led directly to the windpipe and lungs.

David retched but kept his composure; a white wall of sickening emotion had hit him like a tidal wave.

“Identification?” David managed to groan out from underneath his hand-covered mouth.

“Nothing so far. Dental records have shown nothing. No match in DNA, and his fingerprints......”

With a latex-gloved hand, she showed the detective. No skin. Nothing. Just the revealed bareness of his hand, the being's fingertip bones protruded from the open wounds like bloody icicles on a frosted window sill.

“Toxicology report was the most useful evidence so far. Have you heard of Scopolamine?”

David shook his head.

“I would have been surprised if you had. It is a compound that comes from the Brugmansia plant. Native languages call it the “Angels Trumpet” because of its shape. A less friendly name is “Devil's Breath”.

David wondered where this was going. As intelligent and beautiful as she was, Patricia had the unfortunate habit of going off on tangents that were off-topic during conversation.

"You ever wonder where the myth of zombies comes from? It's from this shit. You grind the seeds and pollen together, and it creates dust. Feed this to someone, inject it, blow it in their face, whatever; it does two things. One, it reduces your heart rate to almost nothing; the pulse is barely detectable. Two, it makes you highly susceptible. Urban myths in Columbia range from criminals using this stuff to have you withdraw money from your bank and hand it over to them. Another tale tells of a person who chopped out their kidney for the cartel to sell on the black market. I always thought they were purely made-up horror stories until now. The tox report shows that his blood is full of the stuff."

David's pulse raced to a million miles a second. Absolute pure rage began to course through his veins. Whoever had done this to this being was the epitome of evil, the height of depravity. They needed to be brought down, and it needed to happen right fucking now.

Gritting his teeth together, he muttered, “Thank you, Doctor.”

“David, don't let this get under your skin like I know it can. It's hard. You have to be strong.”

David managed to perform a wrinkled smile to the coroner; its intent was severely lacking in genuineness, and its attempt did not settle Patricia’s nerves in the slightest.

Turning away, he left the icy cold room and began to walk to his desk. He quickly scrawled the time-out sheet, his pace now increasing with each deliberate step.

Reaching the bullpen, he moved over to his desk. Opening a drawer within it, he removed three things.

A torch, a box of bullets and a set of brass knuckles.

Just as he was about to leave, his phone on the desk rang.

Without thinking, he picked up the receiver, a reflex action, a pure Pavlovian response.

"Garston, Homicide, Badge 5278" he barked quickly.

A rough and grumbled voice emanated from the earpiece; it was a voice he recognised immediately.

"David. A pleasure to speak to you. I hope all is well?"

Lee Harper, District Attorney for the city, held the other side of the line, awaiting a response.

"I think you already know the answer to that, Sir."

David scowled at the idea of calling him that authoritative title. It was a necessary evil, unfortunately; a title of privilege, a word of strength given to those with more "valued" jobs.

"Yes, I do know the answer to that."

He replied in a snap; Lee could sense the tone of David's hostile voice.

"That's the reason I called. Your department. It lacks.....leadership. I trust you were there for that charade of a press meeting just now?"

"I was there....."

"You can't deny, then, that Terri did an awful job. I mean, really. A Chief of Police who can't hold a press conference confidently? It's just not acceptable." There was a slight mirth to his voice as if he was stifling a laugh.

"What are you getting at Mr Harper, Sir?

The word “Sir” snapped out of David's mouth, carrying again a sting of venom that punctuated the end of the term.

“What I’m getting at Dave…..”

He hated anyone calling him the short version of his name, and he knew that Lee knew it, too. He was toying with David now, and it made his blood boil.

“What I’m getting at is that we need a change. Now, I know we haven’t always seen eye to eye, but I can leave that water under the bridge and move on. What I think is that Terri has had her day. She needs to leave before she disgraces herself and her squad. You should be the one to replace her.”

David’s mind temporarily slipped to the idea of himself as Captain. He would be lying if it wasn’t a position he aspired for; David simply assumed he would never achieve it. The top people in charge, the DA being one of them, would never allow it.

“I will see to it that you have my full support, and there should be no issue at all in you attaining the position.”

David felt guilty after even considering it for the shortest of seconds.

The anger rose inside him; it was at a fever pitch.

“With all respect, sir,”

The word was now softly spoken, inviting an open ear to listen closer.

“FUCK YOURSELF”

He yelled down the receiver before slamming it back into its holster.

He rose from his desk and moved onwards to the elevator.

The anger within David's mind was palpable; as he passed the uniformed officers in the hall, they moved to one side immediately lest they were run over by this wild stampeding animal. He made his way to the garage.

His car, still nestled in its parking space from the day before, had its keys inserted into the door and then the ignition.

The 8-track and radio spluttered into life....

“T T T T T R G S.... the REAL GREATEST STATION”

David slammed his fist into the plastic-coated metal console, shutting it up once and for all. It broke the skin on his knuckles and drew the slightest hint of blood.

“FUCK IT”

He turned the engine over, his hand stinging full of pain as he drove with furious intent towards his aim, his mission, his calling.

After 10 minutes, he arrived.

Vincenzo’s.

The side alleyway next to the dive bar was scuttled with vermin and torn-apart garbage bags, the brick walls holding fire escapes that clung to the side of the buildings like a spider's web. A single steel door with a slotted sliding peephole was sunk into a niche of the side street. He approached with purpose. He held open handcuffs in one hand, and with the other, he lifted a tightened fist and knocked the tapping tune "Shave and a haircut".

Shortly after, two raps replied, "Two bits".

David spoke confidently, "3. 6. 9. 12."

A suppressed voice from the other side proclaimed, "Welcome, Sibling".

Clink, thunk, slam, rap, tick tick tick tick. CLUNK. A plethora of locks and bolts slid unlocked as the door slowly opened.

David shifted his weight onto his heels and pushed with wrathful force and exertion. A sickening crash cavalcaded into the thin passageway; it was the sound of flesh and bone being crushed.

Entering the dimly lit hall, he saw behind the door a large, well-built man; he was knocked out cold, and his nose was shattered in fragments. He pulled the man's hands together behind his back and handcuffed him tightly.

David pulled the pair of brass knuckles out of his coat pocket and adorned them; a perfect fit.

With one brutal punch, he knocked a tooth out of the jaw of the man now lying on the floor beneath him.

"Don't go anywhere now." He said to the unconscious figure before closing the door behind him again, locking it a dozen times.

Above him, flickering strip lights barely clung to life; they led him further down the long corridor.

After a short walk, he approached a sizeable circular junction with six massive and imposing doors.

Each of them had intricately etched sigils carved into them.

The first door on the left held an eagle with its wings spread open, fluttering in the wind. It was split in two.

The second was a bull emitting steam from its nostrils; the skin on its flank was peeled back like old, tattered wallpaper.

The third is a lion. Bloodthirsty and vengeful, its teeth were dripping full of blood.

The fourth is a snake eating its tail. A serpentine pretzel of hungered knots.

The fifth is a human face. It was the visage of a superbly beautiful woman, her eyes full of tears.

The sixth, directly in front of him, stood a combination of all five. A sphinx, its huge paw held high above its head in salute to a pristinely polished brass sun.

David's stomach dropped as his mind raced to a thousand kilometres an hour.

The eagle split down the middle.

The bull with skin flayed.

He was here. This is where it was orchestrated. This is where the gruesome puzzle was concocted.

David reached into his pocket, grabbed his cellphone, and he pressed and held the number "3". Speed dialling directly to police response, a voice chirped "Headquarters."

"Detective Garston, badge 5278. Seeking back-up 10-78 at the side alley of Maine & Juno."

"Situation?"

"Controlled. 10-26, detained subject relating to case file.....stand by 10-12"

He quickly found his notepad, tattered and folded in his pocket.

"Case file 150704 dash Yankee Oscar Uniform."

A few moments passed.

"10-4, Detective. It's a busy morning, but you will have two squads there ASAP."

"Roger. 10-3."

He moved into the vast circular room holding six doors. He composed himself as he made ready his plan of advancement.

He approached the eagle door and pushed. It held fast. A heavy grunt of disapproval from him was, in turn, matched with a slight sound of something solid falling into place emanating from the door. He surveyed the solid oak barricade before him and noticed a keyhole. It was unusual because it looked like it was designed to unlock with three keys, three slots merged in the same recess.

Walking to the bull door, he saw the same, but with six.

The lion's door, 9. The snakes, 12. The lady's, 15.

But the door that held the sphinx sigil, now directly in front of him, had no keyholes.

His stomach flipped in apprehension as he held his ear next to the boundary in front of him.

It was a noise as close to silence as possible; it edged on the steep of emptiness, but not quite. A slow thrum, a circadian hubble of energy was beyond. Bubbles faintly popped, and water droplets drizzled.

His anxiety began to rise, a slow building of emotion and vicious unease. Fighting to push this aside, he concentrated on his task. He touched the door and caressed the warm wood fibres with his fingers. He propelled gently, and the door creaked open with ease.

A shotgun blast of shock shook him to his core. He was not ready for what he saw.

David's words echoed in the void of his mind.

He remembered the sorrowful and downcast look on Harry Lloyd's face after he revealed to David his first corpse. It was a look of regret but a proud moment of tutelage.

His mind recalled his pledge.

"I promise you this….."

Chapter 12: Gaea's Prophecy To Saturn

A room lay ahead; silken surfaces were covered in sterile silicone. A steel surgical slab lay in the centre; it was occupied by a body; it was splayed across and lay perfectly still, awake, aware, naked and numb.

A multitude of interfering chemicals ran rampant throughout their body, turning them limp.

CORNUCOPIA

Five hooded figures entered the space, each with towered candles held in hand; the smell of hot wax lingered beneath them. With velvet banners held high, they marched with starched and pristine headdresses that covered their face and eyes; it was a procession driven towards the purity of the procedure. Those not carrying the sigil held wicker parcels, their straps woven together in an immaculate nestling bow. Buried within was a multitude of pungent and pristine flowers. A bunch, a bouquet, a garland of foliage, mingled together in a pile permeating their pollen-based perfume across the scene.

Placing their offerings around the circumference of the slab, they blessed it. Speaking in waves, they proclaim it as their altar.

"And so it has come to be. A sibling, not unlike Judas before, has betrayed us."

The man, barely 30 years old, his face full of freckles and hair as red as a scorching flame, lay on the bench. His lip ring shone brightly in reflection of the candle's light; his scrawny body breathed deeply in dulcet tones.

Fred didn't know that the drink poured for him on a salute to the end of his shift would be his last. A shot glass full of shimmering clear liquid tasted ethereal as it passed his tongue and entered his gullet.

Before long, he felt its effects. He realised quickly it was not high-proof booze as promised. After only a singular one-and-a-half-ounce gulp, he felt lighter than air. He tried to stand, but his legs and feet betrayed him. Struggling as he may, he could not move. His tongue lolled uselessly in his mouth, a wet pink slug idling amongst a field of plaque-laden teeth and limp red tastebuds; they sensed nothing.

The group encapsulated him, smothering him, holding him hostage against the frayed fabric booth corner.

"Another one here for our brother."

Fred attempted to protest, but it was useless. He sat still, his weight only being held up by the huddled masses surrounding him. Fred tried pointlessly to stammer even a noise; his body simply would not allow him this simplest of tasks. More alarming than this, he could not feel.

He could sense.

He could smell the damp murk of the bar full of sweat; he could see the billowing clouds of cigarette smoke, neon lights passing through the haze like twitching angelic fingers. He could taste the static buzz of chemicals tap dancing on his palate, mixed with the faintest twinge of bitter almond. He could hear the bass drive of the prominent speakers vibrate through his tympanum; the beat was repetitive and automatic, but he could not FEEL the rumbling of the noise move through his toes like normal. He was numb, painless, yet overwhelmingly aware.

Another silver shot was brought to his table on a rubber tray; it was fading with the emblems of a long-forgotten brewery. A person by his side held his mouth open wide and gaping into the air as an older man, with fingers full of signet rings that each had intricately etched sigils upon them, poured the liquid down his throat.

An icy cold torrent entered his core; as cold as it was, he felt a roping artificial shock run through his skin. An enforcing addition, a forceful entry of ego death flooded his framework.

His quintessence, his very embodiment, felt as if a million rubber stones were subduing and sinking him deeper.

He saw the men on either side of him grab his hands and arms, but he did not physically register it. There was a block. Whatever sense remained, whatever feeling has long since departed. It was peaceful soft, but existentially terrifying.

He succumbed to this as he was carted off, all to the triumphant cries of "Oh - he can't handle it!", "Take him home", "Get him out of here".

The jubilant crowd was quickly excited in the schadenfreude of another drunken soul.

His eyelids, useless and lame, were shuttered by someone's fingertips; he could feel himself moving suddenly, his weight being propelled forward into a soft leather congregation of seats.

He heard the turn of a key, people piling into the vehicle, and an engine roaring into gear, all mingled with the smell of "New Car" tree scent.

Time passed. He heard the wheels of the machine matching the tarmac against his open ears. With no reference, he sank into himself and began to dream.

A giant eagle carried him on soft feathered wings across the horizon, landing softly in a pillow of anaesthesia. He stood before a monumental building, hundreds if not thousands of feet tall, a concrete monument. He saw before him a bull, arrows piercing its sides; he rode upon it using the cruel shrapnel as footrests towards the cascading cement tower. He dismounted and pushed a door open wide; a library, grandiose and expansive, stood before him. In the centre was a solid metal table at hip height. He felt himself being lifted onto it, floating gently, his back lying flat against the cool surface.

Outside of the vision, the natural world was watching. Three shrouded figures surrounded the now naked body of the bartender. Their eyes, cheeks and noses were covered by greying white alabaster; sigils and ancient script scratched into them in deep blushing reds and purples. Their mouths were uncovered; their lips were plump, and their mouths drooled.

From the heart of the room, hidden, a voice spoke in muffled and artificial drones.

“I promise, I engage, and I swear never to reveal the secrets which shall be imparted to me in this temple and blindly to obey my superior.”

A fourth walks in front, holding the sign of their faith aloft, shining bright even in the shaded surroundings. They spoke imposingly as the rest listened carefully. The Master had the attention of the congregation. A meeting of minds. A joining of secret souls.

"And so it is known that in death, the sinners are excluded from eternal paradise and cast into the pit, of which there are nine chambers. The first is for Virtuous unbelievers. The second is for the lustful. The third for the gluttonous. The fourth is reserved for the greedy. The fifth for the wrathful. The sixth for Heretics. The seventh for the brutal. The eighth is for those who are fraudulent. But the deepest and worst circle is reserved for the treacherous. The betrayers, the turncoats. The circle is called Cocytus; the guilty are trapped in ice for eternity. Their tears freeze in their eye sockets, sealing them shut with sharp crystals so that even the comfort of weeping is removed."

The figure moved forward and placed a hand on the bare pectoral muscle of the red-haired specimen before them. They could feel the rise and fall of his lungs, along with the faintest feeling of a beating pulse beneath their fingers.

"I thus breathe upon you to cause truths possessed by us to germinate and penetrate within your heart; I breathe you to fortify your spiritual part; I breathe upon you to confirm you in the faith of your brothers and sisters, according to the engagements you have contracted."

A look of contempt flooded the Masters' face, their thin lips upturned in disgust at the sight of a betrayer.

"And so siblings, we must continue our work, even if members of our own family betray us. Moving forward, we rend and tear the flesh before consuming it, as only in this act are the betrayers allowed to begin their redemption, their journey towards salvation in the eyes of our Holy Mother, full of grace."

The Master invited the crowd to surround the body, still deep in the throes of anaesthesia.

"I swear before the Eternal God of the Grand Mistress and all who hear me, never to write, or cause to be written anything that shall pass under my eyes, condemning myself in the event of impudence to be punished according to the laws of the grand founders, and of all my superiors."

The crowd erupted, a screaming frenzy of approval. A hungry and sharp group of gnashing teeth proceeded onto the deceitful, soon-to-be-redeemed, only if thought to be worthy and willing in the eyes of the Holy Mother.

"HAIL....HAIL....HAIL....HAIL..."

The first bite struck the bicep; the meat of raw human flesh did not falter quickly. With catastrophic force, the absolver, the judge, the jury and the executioner gnawed deeply, removing a huge chunk of meat from the body in front of them. The raw fleshy bite lingered in their teeth; it erupted a surge of blood and plasma across the mask and face to the servant of the Holy Mother, full of grace.

They imagined the beast inside of them encapsulating and engulfing them. A ravaging primal urge to consume, to absorb their prey. The wriggling totem of life beneath them pulsated slowly, the painless admission of their sin washing across them in a haze of hushed gyration.

This was their offering: a singular living, breathing unit ready for consumption.

The pack of the crowd eagerly followed suit, a cackle of predators now primed and ready.

Bloodthirsty and ravenous.

A hundred and twenty-eight human teeth began to feast on the body. Their cheeks and mouths quickly became soaked through with blood; they chewed and ground at the muscley raw flesh under them. Fred barely clung to consciousness as the seventh thrashing bite ripped the skin off the bone. He was beginning to bleed out; his very life force bent, drained and suckled from him. There was no pain, no suffering.

He imagined it was a dream. It must be. He imagined watching a lion in the delta of the plains of Africa being torn asunder by a pack of giggling Hyenas. Howling with mirth at every joyous mouthful they took, the lifeless feline huffed in resignation that the apex predator could still be defeated by a collaborative group of hatred.

The lights on his life failed quickly. His last heartbeat emitted one final burst of blood, which erupted from the dozens of gaping wounds now strewn across his body. His last breath was tired and defeated.

At this, the group withdrew; their task was now complete. Their chops dripped, their pulses slowed, and their temperatures cooled.

The Master spoke, wiping blood from the bottom of their jaw with the cuff of their long grey robe.

"And so now our second pillar is built. It stands parallel with its twin, towering above the foundations already cemented and laid, cut down with reverent mercy and care. One offering of suffering. Two of retribution. Three more are yet to arrive. Thus, we pray, serve, and convene once more for the absolution of this world in preparation for a downpour to erase the sinners from this life, leaving it clean and pure for our purposes. And so we hail."

The Master exited the room, all to a thundering approval of screaming devotion.

"HAIL.... HAIL.... HAIL....HAIL"

Chapter 13: The Thin Blue Line

David Garston waited at the entrance, tapping his feet; he checked his watch and surveyed the concussed body on the ground who was breathing a light rattling snore. Still helpless underneath him, he reared his leg and delivered a kick toe-first into the unconscious man; it was a thunderous and cruel strike full of vitriol.

"Fucker. You'll get what you deserve."

The body coughed, spluttering up blood and teeth in their exhale. They began to speak.

"You should have listened."

The man spoke in pained tones, barely able to expel a sound, but David still heard it as clear as day. The sentiment sent a cold shiver of fear through his body even though the oppressive heat of the desert sun was beating full and hard.

He meandered patiently until two squad cars arrived a few minutes later. Captain Cauldwell exited the first with a plain-clothed CSI in tow. Andrew Liston.

They met each other's eyes and nodded a welcome to one another, not needing to exchange verbal pleasantries.

From the other car, alone, Jake Williams stepped out and strode forward wearing his usual attire of smart shoes and black uniform standard trousers; the only thing that differed was his shirt; usually, it was perfectly crease-free and stainless. David noticed it had been ruffled as if he had been struggling or wrestling against something.

The Captain noticed him; she turned and blocked him with a stiffened forearm.

She gave a stern look; it was not to be taken lightly.

"Jake, I don't think you should be here", voicing her opinion heavily.

Ignoring her completely, he moved past her assertively.

“Show me.”

Jacob was not asking.

He was telling.

He was demanding.

David made a sideway glance to The Captain, who in turn shrugged her shoulders in resignation.

"Such a shame.....in any case, it's your choice, Detective, you're the lead."

David nodded and made his decision quickly.

“Liston. Detain the man handcuffed behind the door. He's currently incapacitated. Captain, you need to see what is in here. Jake........ You make up your mind. I’m not your babysitter. But I agree with Captain. It’s too soon for you to see this.”

The captain nodded in approval before moving forward.

“Take point, David.”

Acknowledging the instruction, he moved the group onwards, taking the squad's lead.

Moving past the open steel door, Liston lifted the man by his handcuffed arms before hauling him; the culprit's feet dragged behind him into the back of the police cruiser.

David led Jacob and The Captain through the long passageway into the vast circular chamber far in the distance.

The Captain and Jacob walked closely behind him, observing his every step closely.

“These doors are locked. We need to get them open ASAP.”

David moved forward to the door that held the visage of the sphinx and pushed, revealing its contents to the awaiting squad.

The solid door opened, and before the officers lay a small room; there were 5 pictures, each hung and framed in intricately carved wooden borders; pinned to each was a tarot card.

The first picture was of a young man with a scalp of strawberry blonde hair; in the picture, it was dyed in a sweeping fringe of pale bottle green. The eyes of the photograph had been scratched out with something sharp. The photo was torn neatly in two straight down the middle from top to bottom.

Pinned to the middle of the ripped picture was a card which depicted a yellowing skeleton in black armour riding a pale horse. It carried a black sigil with a 5-point white rose. The card read: DEATH.

The second picture was a proud police officer. They had just passed their exam; their cap was worn proudly as their chest puffed in self-admiration. Jacob recognised it in an instant, even though the photograph had been disfigured. It was. The face had been erased; it was a whitened silhouette, a pale shadow of pride.

Pinned to the picture was a card that depicted an angel in the heavens blowing a horn downwards onto six naked figures; their lower half was stuck in coffins, and their arms were open wide in reverent acceptance. The card read: JUDGEMENT.

The third picture showed a young man with fiery red hair and a hoop lip piercing. He held no smile nor a scowl; he looked as if the world's troubles had left him numb. The picture had 3 deliberate gaping holes as if a starving animal had attempted to devour it.

Pinned to the picture was a card in bright yellow. On it was an adolescent figure holding a stick and bindle; he was wearing a floral decorative garb with bright orange fiery cuffs, and he had a white rose in his other fist. He was perched on the edge of a cliff, dancing without care. The card read: THE FOOL.

The fourth was a distant picture taken from afar. It was a man in plain clothes, a light tan coat and blue jeans. His hair was brushed back in a swooping brown wave. It was a candid photo of David Garston. The picture had not been altered or touched. No damage was yet done to it.

Pinned to the picture was a card; it showed an older man in a long hooded grey cape walking on clouds; his beard was as white as snow. In one hand, he held a long silver walking staff, and in the other was a lantern glowing golden in the foggy ether. The card read: THE HERMIT.

The fifth was a picture of a female dressed in a police uniform. Several sparkling badges shone, pristinely polished. Flecks of long blonde hair flowed from her scalp. The face of the photograph had been completely extinguished; a blatant bullet hole masked the portrait. The three officers knew automatically who it was. It was the picture that they saw every day as they entered work. It was Captain Terri Cauldwell.

Pinned to the picture was a card; it showed a woman between two pillars, one jet black and one ebony white. In her hands, she held a scroll; the writing on it was unintelligible. She wore a long, flowing sky-blue robe; a crown which had a perfect circle upon her head was indented with craters that resembled a full moon. Around her neck was a pendant holding a large crucifix. The card read: THE HIGH PRIESTESS.

In front of the pictures were two things lying reverently on a raised dais.

The first was a chapter from the Holy Bible that rested spread-eagled across two tissue-thin sheets of paper. The heading read "Revelations 6".

“And I saw when the Lamb opened one of the seals, and I heard as it were the noise of thunder, one of the four beasts saying, "Come and see". And I saw; and beheld a white horse: and he that sat on him had a bow, and a crown was given unto him. And he went forth conquering and to conquer."

"And when he had opened the second seal, I heard the second beast say, "Come and see".
And there went out another horse that was red: and power was given to him that sat thereon to take peace from the earth and that they should kill one another: and there was given unto him a great sword.

And when he had opened the third seal, I heard the third beast say, "Come and see". And I beheld a black horse, and he that sat on him had a pair of balances in his hand.

And when he had opened the fourth seal, I heard the voice of the fourth beast say, "Come and see". And I looked and beheld a pale horse: and his name that sat on him was Death, and Hell followed with him.

And power was given unto them over the fourth part of the earth to kill with sword, with hunger, with death and with the beasts of the world.

And when he had opened the fifth seal, I saw under the altar the souls of them that were slain for the word of God and for the testimony which they held.

And they cried with a loud voice saying, "How long, O Lord, holy and true, dost thou not judge and avenge our blood on them that dwell on the earth?"

And white robes were given unto every one of them; and it was said unto them that they should rest yet for a little season until their fellow servants and their brethren should be killed as they were and they shall be fulfilled.

And I beheld when they opened the sixth seal and, lo, there was a great earthquake; and the sun became black of night, the moon became as blood, and the stars of heaven fell unto the earth, even as a fig tree casteth her untimely figs when she is shaken of a mighty wind.

And the heaven departed as a scroll when it is rolled together, and every mountain and island were moved out of their places. And the kings of the earth, the great men, the rich men, the chief captains, the mighty men, every bondman and every free man hid themselves in the dens and in the rocks of the mountains; And said to the mountains and rocks, "Fall on us, and hide us from the face of them that sitteth on the throne, and from the wrath of the Lamb."

For the great day of wrath has come, and who shall be able to stand?"

The second sheet of paper was a large map; stretched and unravelled, it was pinned with rusted nails to the platform.

It is a map of the valley and the surrounding city borough. Etched with a wide-edged red marker is a perfect circle with one dot in the centre. It lay on the outskirts, around 300 kilometres from the city centre, far away from the strip nestled in a verdant forest uphill. Around the edges of the circle were glyphs, ancient and primordial. Written steadily is a date; it is today's date, as clear as a bell. Alongside it was a time. 23:58. Two minutes to midnight.

In the corner of the room stood a large refrigerator with an open door. Inside were dozens of beakers filled with various coloured liquids plastic bags containing powder, pills and dried leaves. It was a miasma of drugs; it was enough to supply thousands.

Captain Cauldwell stood stiff as a board; her skin had turned even paler than usual, and her eyes and soul had transformed into grey, lifeless matter. She wandered back to the front door, waving at David and Jacob to follow.

They walked together in silence.

“David, Jacob.......” She spoke slowly, her face as white as a sheet; her body hobbled listlessly. It was as if she had seen a ghost, and by all accounts, she had. It was her own.

"I'm placing myself and both of you in protective custody ASAP. Targets have been put on our backs. They know who we are, and they know where we live. They have a goal, and they will stop at nothing to achieve it. I recommend you two stay together for at least the next 4 days. Do not attempt to move or go ANYWHERE. I will do the same with Detective Liston. Look after each other, stay in contact, and for god's sake, stay safe."

The Captain removed a cell phone from a holster on her side, flipping it open before pressing a series of digits.

"Badge number "3598; Captain Cauldwell. Code 2, seeking immediate locations of two available safehouses.”

The Captain shifted her weight on her heels anxiously as she awaited a response.

“Roger. 10-23."

She shifted the cell phone, which rested between her ear and raised shoulder, as she jotted a note on her standard-issue sketchpad.

"Asking for a 10-9 on that 10-20...... Ok. Officers 10-76 immediately."

She pulled the note from the pad and handed it to David. Written on it in hurried handwriting was an address; it was a hotel a few miles away.

She wrote a second note and placed it in her breast pocket before hanging up the phone and putting it back in its leather nest.

She spoke with serious intent to David and Jacob; it was a tone of voice that held no quarter.

"I'm transferring this to the major crimes division. It's no longer in your hands. Move out."

Jacob's teeth audibly clenched.

"Absolute fucking horse shit, out of my hands. These people have made it my business."

Jacob was furious, his teeth almost bursting at the pressure of his shut jaw. His hands were turning a strangled shade of white with how hard he made an unthrown fist.

"THAT'S ENOUGH DETECTIVE. STAND. DOWN."

Captain Cauldwell was not taking no for an answer this time. She was rarely one to ever raise her voice, but when she did, you knew to fucking listen.

David took hold of Jacob's shoulder and pulled him towards him, embracing him in his arms. Jacob could smell his aftershave; it was musky and citric, and he unsuccessfully attempted to mask his unshowered odour from the night before.

David whispered to him.

"Trust me. Take my lead."

He held on for a touch longer, pressing Jacob's head into his chest more firmly.

“Good. Now pull away and pretend to wipe a tear from your eye, then shake my hand."

Jake followed the instructions to a tee.

David noticed that the Captain was looking at them; it was just as he had intended.

"We're good now, Captain. Aren't we, Jake?"

"Yeah. We're good."

Captain Cauldwell nodded quickly in approval.

"Keep in contact at least twice a day."

She entered the police car and drove off with Detective Liston. As they pulled away, the perp handcuffed in the backseat raised their head from their lap, made eye contact and winked at them as they pulled away into the distance.

David knew major crimes would be here any second now, so he moved quickly. He ran down the corridor and into the circular chamber before grabbing the map from the table; he stuffed it hurriedly into his coat pocket. Running quicker, he exited the hall and back into the alleyway.

"Get in the car, quick. Go, go, go."

David instructed Jake in urgency.

David could hear the sound of sirens getting closer now, so he quickly jumped into his car; he turned on the ignition and stepped on it.

Jacob was jostled; his mind was still reeling.

"Why the rush?"

"Because if major crimes arrived and we were still there, they'd have our asses."

Jake shrugged at the response. It wouldn't be the first time they would have been admonished for bending the rules.

"And because if they saw that something was missing….."

David threw the crumpled map into Jake's lap.

"They'd fire us in a heartbeat for tampering with evidence."

A momentary beat was shared between the two officers.

The engine roared as David drove down the strip way above the limit.

"You see, Jake, I think you're right. They have made it our business. They have made it personal. Even though I don't think you're ready yet, you're right."

Jake saw David's brow, still dripping in sweat, was furrowed in exerted purpose.

"Let's tear this thing to the fucking ground."

Jake nodded as he silently pointed to David to make the next left turn.

"We're almost at the end of this, Jake."

The smell of burning rubber and gasoline smoke returned the memory of David's first chase; it was shared with his mentor, his guardian.

" I promise you this….."

Chapter 14: Sic Semper Tyrannis

Detective Andrew Liston and Captain Terri Cauldwell began the half hour drive towards Police Headquarters. The Captain took control of the vehicle as Liston sat next to the wounded man in the back seat.

Since apprehending the as-of-yet unidentified perp, Andrew could not fail to notice that the look on their face had not changed.

A smirk.

His eye was bulged, sore and beginning to blacken and his mouth was bloody and battered. But still, his lips were upturned in a smug grin.

Andrew had to remain calm. His temper sometimes got the better of him, but he knew that with the Captain driving upfront, he could not afford any slip-ups, even on the most minor scale; the case was personal to her now, and he knew that her life was on the line.

The perp squirmed, shifting his weight in the seat of the police cruiser.

"Keep still, or I will be forced to physically keep you still."

Andrew spoke directly and to the point, using a tone similar to when a parent admonishes a naughty child.

"Just needed to adjust myself, don't mind me."

Underneath the bruises and blood, Andrew remarked in his mind that the man took his appearance with pride. His beard was groomed perfectly; he smelt expensive aftershave on his neck and saw the slightest hint of mascara to accentuate his eyelashes. He could also see that his smirk had still not faltered. The anger started to get to him now.

"Why are you smiling? You know something I don't?"

The man next to him released a low and quiet chuckle.

"Oh, Detective. I know plenty that you don't."

Before Andrew could react, he heard the noise of something snap. It sounded like a dry twig breaking in half. The man beside him took a huge breath of air into his lungs and closed his eyes.

Within seconds the inside of the car was full of a heavy silver fog. The smell of the man's aftershave was replaced by the scent of mixed chemicals and melting plastic; it stung his eyes and nostril hairs, a slow and vicious burn.

Andrew's perspective shifted almost immediately. He felt the police cruiser sway from side to side as if he were a baby in a hamper. The leather seat beneath him seemed to envelop him like quicksand; it felt warm, comforting and almost sensuous. He felt the pressure of his surroundings change as the darkness around the edges of his vision crept forward as slowly as a spider crawling across its silken web.

He felt now that the vehicle had ceased to move, but he could still hear the engine roar, blasting its acrid smoke into the city air. He tried to focus his sight on the Captain, but her sandy blonde hair was a blur, a weaving cornfield being blown by an invisible wind. His hands waved in front of his face as he tried in vain to find something to concentrate upon. He instead felt himself breaking into an uncontrollable fit of laughter. His fingers looked like uncooked hotdogs fresh from the tin; they wobbled and jiggled together in a huddled, ludicrous mess.

As his laughter continued, his body sank deeper and deeper into the recesses of the back seat, looking up at the man he had arrested; Andrew saw now that they had put on a mask. He could hear the man's breath being pushed through a tiny slot where the mouth would usually be; it released a tinny metallic whine upon every exhale. The mask itself only added to the relentless mirth he felt; it is ivory white with red and purple etchings drawn intricately over its visage. It was preposterous. It was unreal. It was the funniest thing he had ever seen, and he did not know why.

In a flash, Andrew felt a shift. His weight was being moved. No longer sinking into the seat, he felt his body fall onto the dusty earth outside. He was completely incapacitated by his spasms of humour; he rolled on the ground like an earthworm seeking out water.
He felt his gun being removed from the holster on his belt.

Something sang out to him.

"Thank you for this generous gift", drifted from the mouth of the man now standing above him. He saw the masked figure turn the gun to the Captain in the driver's seat as he moved away. He entered the vehicle, still keeping the pistol raised and pointed at his target. The door slammed shut, and Andrew heard the car pull away into the distance.

It was at that point that the change occurred.

The laughter and joy he felt turned into a million feathers flicking across his skin. It tickled; it was hilarious, but it was excruciating. His face and stomach were cramping from the muscles working overtime, supporting his uncontrollable mirth. He felt the fibres of the imaginary goose feathers enter his skin and into his bloodstream. Within seconds, his body was shaking. Every tendon, vein and artery began to pop up from his skin, carrying the itch across and along his whole self.

His teeth clenched hard, scrunching up in his mouth with an audible squeaking noise, his molars and incisors were on the verge of exploding in his jaws. He began to scratch himself to try and alleviate the sensation, but it was to no avail.

Once he started this, however, he found himself physically unable to stop. Within a minute, his body was red raw with fingernail marks, and within two, he was drawing blood.

His sanity dropped; he could see dancing kaleidoscopic visions of angels descending from the heavens; it made him weep pained tears as he continued endlessly gnawing at his skin with his fingertips. It simply wasn't doing the trick. In his delirium, he found a stone, rough with gnarled and pointy edges.

Picking it up, he rubbed it against his arms, legs and face. Waves of relief flooded his core as his trembling hands grazed the scraping stone across his exposed muscles. He felt the warmth of his blood covering his hands as his vision faded to blackness.

Andrew Liston's last thoughts before he perished were of his ex-wife and the life and stories he could have shared with her if only he could have made the time to do so.

Tempus Fugit.

Chapter 15: By The Pricking Of Our Thumbs

Deep green pine needles appeared almost black and blue in the smog-filled night sky; they were hanging from tall but skinny, withered tree limbs. The scent of petrichor was profuse; it was a temporary antidote to the soul, a band-aid that barely covered a wide-open wound of dread.

David parked his car on the side of the road and stepped out with Jake in tow. They stepped onto the damp earth and began to search, to seek out something, anything in the dense thickets of the overgrowth.

After almost an hour, Jake saw a practically imperceptible footpath, a welcome mat into the pitch-black maze of nature.

With flashlights in hand, they began to walk the dark passageway, the road unknown.

Their torches illuminated twisted branches as they cautiously ventured deep into the plantation; the ominous silence was broken only by the rustling of leaves and breaking twigs underfoot.

As they ambled deeper, a sense of unease settled in their stomachs. The towering trees and vines cast long, dark, shifting shadows that swallowed everything around them. The soft rusting of leaves whispered secrets only nature itself could understand.

With every passing moment, the forest took a tighter grip.

By the first 5 minutes, they knew that without the map, they would have been lost almost immediately, and their sense of direction became increasingly uncertain. The dense trees and underbrush seemed to close around them, obscuring recognisable landmarks. As their torches flickered in the oppressive darkness, they continued step by step, carefully.

By 30 minutes, their breaths had become laboured; their paces halted to a baby's crawl. Any remnant of a trail was now far away in the distance; they walked through the thickets and the foliage; it was a living and breathing labyrinth of emerald coppice.

They could hear now the distant calls of unfamiliar creatures and the faintest rush of a hidden stream. Their hearts pounded as they trudged on, determined yet yearning for the comfort of civilisation. Surveying the map to no avail, they were searching for something, anything.

They continued onwards into the ever-growing murk of the forest. Panic threatened to consume them both in the everlasting vast sea of green. Everything appeared identical; every moss-covered rock was a cruel mockery of the last. A master of deception, it is a place where time stood still, and the boundaries of reality and imagination blurred. Deep down, they knew their journey, although uncertain, also held the promise of discovery and redemption. For as they both knew, it is sometimes deep within the unknown that you can find what you truly seek.

By the hour mark, they saw the faintest sliver of light in the distance: a beacon of hope shining, a radiant star glowing, beckoning them and summoning them forth. They switched off their torches and proceeded on; their paces quickened by the discovery.

As they drew closer, they saw a giant building lit by a single flickering light bulb. It was derelict and decrepit; only a handful of windows remained out of the hundreds that would have once adorned the massive concrete behemoth.

Several towers scattered around the vicinity of the central hub, most of them crumbled and broken to dust. Once there had been life here, it would have been a bustling hub of industry churning with activity, but this had long since departed, leaving behind an empty shell now covered with creeper vines, ivy and nightshade.

CORNUCOPIA

Two wooden posts, splintered and moss-covered, supported a large sign. Faded, warped and scratchy letters had been written onto it several decades ago.

"Briswell County Water Plant"

David had lived here for almost twenty-five years and had never heard of it. He remembers vaguely that the county itself no longer existed; it had merged with the larger and more populated county adjacent. It was so long ago he barely clung to the memory.

From somewhere deep within the bowels of the building, softly and slowly, an echoing bass drum thumped four times, followed by a distant series of chants. Then, a noise that was unlike anything he had heard before. It started low and dull but resolved itself into a shrill scream. It was inhuman, otherworldly and in life, leeching amounts of pain.

Moving forward, they crept through the bushes towards the commercial fortress, closing in nearer and nearer with every laboured silent step, heavy with hushed exertion.

As they drew close to the wide-open gateway, another set of drums bellowed from inside. This time, five snares snapped in repetition: the death march. The hairs on their arms stood as straight as corn in a field; a shiver stood on the precipice of dread.

They entered the looming structure with knees bent and arms forward, stalking the sound from within like primed and ready predators eager to catch their prey. Little did they know that they were the ones who were being hunted.

The tumbled dusty pillars of the entryway sprouted with twisted and torn supporting wires; they crept through the broken and torn asphalt like ingrown hairs bursting through the epidermis of scarred skin.

The complex was imposing from a distance, but walking inside was another thing altogether. A barren web of corridors and passageways lay ahead of them; the walls, ceiling and mezzanines were covered with an innumerable untold legion of pipes, conduits and channels. They were the veins and arteries of a long-since-dead industrial colossus; they knew that the answer must lay at the centre, the heart.

The pitch-black depths of the building quickly became sickening, a resounding reminder of the desolate nature of life itself. They were frigid inside but still perspired with fear. The sight of the ducts and tubes leaking fluid started to resemble icy pendulums, stalactites once holding the lifeblood of a long-since departed society.

Jake withdrew a Zippo lighter from a small pocket on his side, clicked open the lid and struck the flint wheel. A small burst of flame shone alongside the aroma of burning petrol; it gave a temporary respite from the oppressive bleakness. The relief was only momentary. The fire lit up within his cupped hand and shone across the walls of the endless corridor. What was previously hidden was now revealed. It was Dark and crude writing as if it had been written by a shaking fingertip. Scrawled on the cement is something that was once hidden by the blackness; it is now illuminated and painfully clear.

"He gurgled for air as his windpipe was split."

"The last words from his mouth were him begging for his mother."

"He skinned himself alive willingly as you watched, unhelping."

"A glorious suicide provoked and prodded by our willing hand."

"Our lips and teeth are like bloodied needles; the feast has been completed."

"Onwards you travel, deeper into our work, still clueless about what is to come."

"Your lives are now worthless; you will become part of our process for the power and the glory evermore."

David noticed Jake was shaking. His hands were clenched in tight, skinny fists; they were pierced with white exertion. The veins on the temple of his brow bulged, and his rage was barely suppressed. His knees were tense like a coiled spring.

A low murmur flew through the corridors; it was a chant of four words screamed from the far distance.

"HAIL.....HAIL.....HAIL.....HAIL...."

"Fuck this"

Jake burst into a sprint. Rocketing ahead, he ran with lung-bursting urgency towards the voices. He was at least a hundred metres away when David turned and began to chase after him.

"What the fuck are you doing? Stick together, kid."

David yelled into the distance but was ignored as Jake gained momentum. His young muscles were much quicker and more robust than David's. Jake pulled away into the abyss, drowning himself in the dark, and he fell quickly out of sight.

David slowly trotted down to a jog, huffing and wheezing until he was at a laboured slow step. His knees had given in, and his lungs burned as he gasped for air.

"For fucks sake, kid. What are you doing?"

A rasping artificial voice full of malice replied to his question from behind him.

"*NOTHING YOU WOULDN'T DO IF YOU COULD HAVE.*"

His mouth and nose were forcibly covered by a damp and scratchy rag that smelled of pear drops and sulphur.

A low, vicious chuckle rang down into David's eardrum. His vision soon spiralled into a cacophony of lights and colours, a magnificent kaleidoscope of flashing energy exploding and colliding.

Fractals spun and circled, and a soft wave of sleep began to envelop him from his lungs and onwards into his limbs and brain. As his eyelids fluttered shut and his consciousness dropped, the same voice taunted him, sending him into a fever dream of dread.

"*YOU SHOULD HAVE LISTENED....*"

I promise you this.....

Chapter 16: Blessed Are The Meek

Far within the tangled and dark walls lay a massive wire container covered in black hessian. It bellowed and waved from the deep breaths of the vast being that rested within it. A low growl rumbled from inside the fabric, a guttural stomach-churning barrage of caged brutality. A duo of winches were punched and riveted into the floor. Above was a supporting brace, oiled, lubricated and ready for purpose.

Five figures entered the room; they were a congregation on the march of a funeral procession.

One held a huge bass drum held by straps across their broad and burly shoulders.

One held a snare drum; it was looped by a taught cord that hung around their neck.

One held a long and rock solid spear that was shimmering and pristinely polished, its razor-sharp pointed edge aimed forwards at their target.

One held a rope trail, coiling around their arms in a serpentine embrace, frayed fabric tickling their arms and split ends spread into the nooks of their elbow creases.

The last held a tome that was ancient and as heavy as lead. It was dusty yet well-read, yellowing with age and bluing with aged mould. Glyphs, scripture and prose, were scratched and etched on the cover and pages. It is full of knowledge, wisdom and ultimate evil.

The Master, with a book in hand, read reverently from the scripture aloud. Their voice was altered and distorted by machine; it was robotic, dull and monotone but full of intent and passion.

"Here we stand, my siblings, on the edge. The precipice. The knife's sharp line. The razor blades are stiff and rigid edge, ready to cut this world in two. The pure and the tainted. The holy and the heathens. The just and the guilty."

The Master moved forward and removed the dark cover from the cage, revealing the animal within.

Its fur was as gold as ground cornmeal and thick and tangled as a burrowing spider's nest. Its eyes were as bottomless, glassy, shimmering and everlasting as a play doll. A jaw revealed a hundred snarling teeth, each pin needle-sharp; they are instruments meant to consume flesh. Its comprehensive yet slender body rippled with a thousand toned muscles, each engineered for one purpose. To kill. Their four paws were each as wide as a thick dinner plate, hid vicious claws, a culmination of a million years of selective evolution to create a killing machine.

A lion lay curled in a suppressed circle, its massive and proud body coiled in the tight enclosure.

"The third key signifies the famine to come. We have partaken in the flesh of the convicted and now ready ourselves for the second part of the sacrifice, an offering for our Holy Mother, full of grace, to be reborn, resurrected, wrathful and filled with righteous vengeance to be delivered on the sinners of this world."

The hooded figure who held the spear drew closer, moving through the small line of shrouded humanity wearing the masks of their faith, their faces covered in reverence for their creator, their religion and their god, waiting patiently to be summoned forth once again into this world.

The Master spoke again; their voice crackled with purpose.

“And I saw the dead, great and small, standing before the throne, and two books were opened. One of which is the book of life. The dead were judged according to their actions, as recorded in the books. The sea gave up the dead that was in it, and Death himself returned them to the earth, and each person was judged according to what they had done. Anyone whose name was not found written in the Book of Life was thrown into the lake of fire. The lake of fire is the second death".

The Master nodded at the spear-bearer, inviting them to undergo their purpose.

The joust pointed at the target, and they nodded to their sibling holding the bass drum on their stomach, who observed at the side.

THUMP

The shank of the weapon held tighter in their hands, steadying their nervous, shaking hands.

THUMP

A wave of euphoria entered the souls of the parish, an echoing hit of spiritual exuberance. They knew at this moment that they were righteous.

THUMP

A sharp lunge pushed forward using the tightened muscles of their triceps released a swift and immediate pierce that entered the beast in its stomach, just above the hip. The feeling of the blade entering its flesh sent quivers of pleasure through the spear bearer's nerves, the tiny blonde hairs on their arms erect, alert, wild and electric.

A guttural howl matched the squelch of torn skin and muscle as the spear was twisted within the wound, widening it and spreading the incision outwards. The hooked and curved blade pulled and spilt the intestines and stomach, tumbling outwards onto the cement, splashing blood and entrails covering the plain grey stone.

The beast lay slowly dying on the barren killing floor as the hooded figure that held the long length of rope hobbled forward. Looping and twisting their hands, the shadow formed a knot, unbreakable and solid. It wrapped around the cage ceiling, the other end falling around the gasping monster's neck.

A wire tethered to the ceiling began to lift the cage slowly.

The lion, startled by this, attempted to pounce free but fell instantly; its legs were useless. Another low rumble shook the room's foundations as the cage lifted higher, stopping at 7 feet from the ground.

The rope dangled downwards, and the looping knot clung to the neck of the lion, tightening quickly. The gallows loomed; a military snare pounded, and the noose was ready.

The enclosure ascended to the high ceiling above, winching; it choked the beast as it was lifted underneath the chamber. Struggling and twitching for its last breath, its huge legs kicked and bashed to no effect. The deed had been done, and its destiny was sealed.

The Master inched forward and removed a glove from their right hand. Reaching inside the lions, pouring wet wounds, they grasped, held and pulled. Whatever innards and entrails remained now leaked out in a single sickening tug.

Quoting quietly, they spoke to the eager few who were listening keenly onward.

"The third step is complete; two remain, with one already in progress."

They nodded to a sibling of the cult silently. They knew precisely what to do, and so they stepped into the black distance of an endless corridor adjacent.

"The second pillar of our house has been constructed, awaiting the rafters and roof to be placed high on top. A house for our Holy Mother, full of grace to sit, stay, slumber and ultimately bring an end to this world. A glorious death for the reckless and uncaring sinners, a new haven for the willing, the just, those adhering to our faith. For this will truly be a house for the holy, a bright new dawn sprouting forth from the embers of this dying system."

"HAIL.....HAIL.....HAIL.....HAIL"

The Master adorned their shoulders in the blood of the beast in a symbol of the faith, a runic sigil designed to summon and welcome the goddess with a thousand names. They walked away from the scene with their siblings in tow; they were ready and waiting for the next part of the plan that would soon take place in front of their very eyes.

Chapter 17: Ouroboros

In the inky blackness of his subconscious, David found himself standing at the precipice of a nightmare. Before him lay a labyrinth of unfathomable complexity; its twisting corridors and towering walls were illuminated only by a feeble and flickering liquid gas lighter held by a figure ahead that clutched it with a trembling hand. The air was thick with an oppressive silence that was torn apart by the sounds of their laboured breath and stiffened footsteps.

With each tentative step, he proceeded into the heart of the structure, the walls seemingly closing in around him; the very stone conspired to keep him prisoner in its malevolent embrace. David felt the weight of an unseen presence; it was a malicious force that watched and waited in the shadows; a bitter and evil-minded voice whispered in his ear, willing and urging him deeper into the void.

"YOU SHOULD HAVE LISTENED."

The figures' flame sputtered; it dimmed eerie, elongated cascading shadows that danced across the stone walls.

David sank deeper into his psyche; a lead weight of fear pulled him downwards, quicker and quicker.

His eyes fluttered and flicked open; the scene shifted and halted immediately away from the dark pit he was entering. He found himself now out in the open. It was a bright summer day; the sky was clear and empty of wandering clouds. He felt the familiar weight of his tan coat, but something felt.....different. It was not soft, nor was it pliant. It was stiff, fresh, and spotless. Brand new. He then noticed his hands. The scar from a knife wound a few years back had disappeared. Not only that, his body seemed.....younger.

A familiar voice rang out to him. It was old, weathered and nurturing.

“Come on, kid, may as well rip the band-aid off sooner rather than later.”

A thousand goose pimples erupted on his arm as he turned to look at the person speaking to him.

It was his mentor, his advisor, his guide.

Sergeant Henry Lloyd.

He was the same as he remembered him 25 years ago. His brow was wrinkled and furrowed, and his hair was as fleeting and soft as dying candle smoke. His deep and soulful brown eyes were hidden by an untamed bushel of eyebrow hair that was wirey, pointed and wild. His whitening moustache, which adorned his top lip, was stained slightly yellow by the years of nicotine, decorating his mouth, which seldom frowned. His plain clothes were old and weathered, and his ancient loafers split at the seams.

“Have you ever seen a body before?”

A reply came from David's lips without him prompting it. He was out of control of his movements, speech and faculties, but he still felt everything. Every gust of wind, every lingering scent, every discordant sound.

“No, Sir. But I suppose there's no time like the present.”

Harry nodded solemnly to him, pushing him forward without words.

Intel had told David it was a road accident or a suspected hit-and-run. A young Asian woman who was barely 19 years old.

David walked forward and saw a hive of activity. Officers wore blue paper-like PPE equipment as they snapped photos, took notes and spoke to each other in hushed tones. One stepped to one side for a moment, and it was then that David saw her.

She reminded him of a high school friend whose name he failed to pluck from memory. His eyes were fixed on hers; they were open, unblinking and vacant. He stared for what felt like the longest time. He imagined the life of this young woman and what she could have done or what she could have been. It had been cut short in an instant. A cruel end from an uncaring world.

“Kid…..”

His eyes jolted back from hers, and this was when he noticed what was left of her head. Her jet-black hair was speckled with ebony white skull fragments, all muddied and full of gore. Her brain was spilt out across the asphalt, an organ lying useless and dead.

And then the smell.

A stench of iron and stale meat. Like an abattoir.

His face turned green, and his stomach flipped. Turning around in a rush, he vomited into his own cradled arms, heaving bile and retching spit onto his coat bought only 3 days prior.

A series of chuckles arose from the group behind him before being patted on the back reassuringly.

“It’s ok, Kid. Don't pay any attention to them. They’re broken. They’re anaesthetised to this shit. This shows you’re human. You don’t want to end up like those fucks.” Henry pointed towards the officers, still revelling in the schadenfreude of the newbie. David remembers spending that night, his first of many to come, perched up on the high seat of a bar. David and Henry spoke through the night until daybreak the following morning. He did not recall much, but the one thing he did was what he learned that night.

"There's one thing I know from working all these years. You cannot work in this profession without severing a piece of yourself away. You will never be whole. The public, the officials, the press, and the government will all be against you. It's kill or be killed."

Henry clicked his fingers at the bartender, busy talking to a gaggle of young female students who had just walked in.

The server ignored him and carried on flirting. He made a bunched fist and inhaled white powder into his right nostril.

Henry clicked his tongue, a solid tut, and muttered to David, "Some people just don't fucking listen."

"HEY YOU. GET THE FUCK OVER HERE. NOW."

The server stopped and turned his head, scowling at the voice shouting at him. He moved towards Henry, making sure to let his annoyance known with every heavy step.

"What do you want, old man?"

Henry fired off his trademark wry smile, revealing his yellow tartar-covered teeth.

"You ever have a favourite uncle who had one of those cheesy magic tricks? Here's one for you."

He showed his hands were empty by wriggling his nicotine-stained fingers up at the person watching impatiently.

"I'm going to make our bar tab disappear."

He put his hands down by his sides and unclipped two things from his belt loop before clunking them on the bar top. His gun and his badge.

The bartender nervously twitched as he quickly smudged the chalky substance off his nose.

“Abracadabra. It’s vanished.”

Henry chuckled loudly to himself as he watched the bartender scrunch up a paper ticket that, at the bottom, was totalled at just shy of $200.

“Finish up, David. Long day ahead.”

They moved out of the bar and shook each other's hands in the pouring rain outside.

“You have to promise me, David. Promise me you will always use your heart and not your head.”

David nodded solemnly, the words sinking deep into his very core.

“I promise you this…..”

A flash of blackness cascaded over him.

He was on his knees now, transported back to the bathroom of his apartment that same day. The sun had now set, the sound of sirens from outside endless and constant, a barrage of unfamiliar and unwelcome audio.

He knelt before his toilet and expelled the last of his stomach contents. He had tried to sleep that night but to no avail; the day's occurrences removed that option quickly. So, he drank.

And listened. And drank. And watched. And drank significantly more than he should have until he was where he now resided: poisoned, infected and limp.

Once more, his perspective shifted and altered into darkness.

He could smell something earthy, balmy and sweet. It choked his lungs with its thickness. A long stream of smoke flowed and fell from a ball swinging on a chain held by a white-robed figure. He heard a vibration in the air that was airy yet harsh. An organ breathing in the air before playing long and sorrowful devotion notes. Ahead, a closed casket adorned with a perfectly pressed and folded flag, roses and lilies laid on top. A picture of Bryan Williams stood beside in a sturdy wooden frame. A young man, no more than 16, stumbled slowly towards the oaken box of human remains. Silently, he lay a hand on top and bowed his head.

A few seconds felt like an eternity.

He moved along and sat next to a weeping widow dressed in all black as Terri Cauldwell began to speak.

"Bryan Williams….."

She swept a droplet from her eye, coughing away her scratchy voice, raw from tears.

"Bryan Williams. A Father. A husband. A soldier. A hero. Standing upright for justice, forever. But more than that. A decent human. It's a rare thing these days. It is why the team and I do what we do. To protect and serve. To guard and to watch. As we bid our farewells, please stand with me."

The crowd stood, as did David with them.

"Never forget him. Always remember what he did. For it is in this act that he shall always be alive in our hearts."

Terri stepped to one side as she faced the casket. She bowed for a moment before snapping upright in a salute with white gloves that covered her slim hands.

His vision shifted one last final time. Back to reality, his true nightmare.

He was strapped, arms bent backwards, legs knotted with rough and knotted rope, his chest open and exposed. His back was curved against something solid and ancient. Struggling, with no hope, he opened his eyes. A massive room within the complex was strewn with a hundred or more flickering pillar candles. Stretching his neck around, he saw in front and beneath him a pit with seemingly no end. And then, the mirror.

A perfectly polished silver obelisk revealed to him everything.

He saw himself, beer belly revealed, strapped to a carriage wheel as large as himself, cemented into the earth below, unmoving. His arms were bound tight against the spokes of it, his legs anchored to the ground. Around the wheel, on the floor, interweaving with the candles, was coarse, thick and rocky dust that reeked of sodium. Rock salt. A perfect circle, inside of which were several sigils, symbols and runes made of melted candle wax.

David heard them now. A series of footsteps moving forward. From the shadows loomed a series of figures holding candles in hand. Their faces were obscured by hoods, and what little he could make out was covered by ashen grey masks speckled with red lines and blood spots.

A voice resounded behind him, his eyes skipping to the surprise, and his stomach dropped in dread. A piercing, electric, altered tone spoke.

"Sibling. You may take charge of this offering."

"Thank you, Master." The voice that spoke this was immediately familiar. They stepped in front and removed their mask.

Piercing green eyes. Wide and stocky. His eyes and nose were bloodied. The Bartender.

"Now, before we begin......"

He pointed at his bruised face, his orbital bone a dark, blushing purple.

"An eye for an eye....."

David felt his right eyelid being forced open by the figure behind him, the soft cotton gloves rubbed against his tear duct and eyelash.

The man curled his hand back behind his shoulder like a coiled spring, and released. His arm unfurled, his hand propelling forwards.

A stiffened finger scratched at David's exposed pupil like a whip crack.

David once heard that the eye has no pain receptors. He knew in this instance that this was a lie. It burned and stung like nothing he had felt before; tears and blood ran downwards onto his cheek.

Scrunching his face in agony, he opened his other eye involuntarily.

He saw a hooded figure behind his tormentor pass them something short and metallic.

The bartender pointed to his open mouth; his lip was split and leaking blood. There was a gap where a tooth once lay, now vacant and empty.

"A tooth for a tooth….."

David's mouth was wrenched open suddenly by the same set of gloved hands.

He waved in front of David's face a claw hammer before placing it in his open maw on top of a yellowing incisor on his bottom jaw.

The feeling of the nerve ending being severed within his gums sent sickening electric shocks of pure agony throughout his face. With two gut-wrenching twists, the tooth came loose in a half chunk of bone and spittle.

David screamed in pain, spraying blood across the room in anguish. The fog of the drugs now completely waned; all that was left was suffering and liquid red-hot fury.

He felt the ropes around his arms tighten slightly; the fibres creaked and groaned.

The figure behind him marched forward, and with each step, his bonds squeezed tighter and tighter still. His wrists turned pale white, his fingers expanding with popped veins.

A shout, a scream, a profession of passion, all from the innards of these people. A wave of pure denomination, a clique serving a personal god with ultimate love.

"HAIL OUR MOTHER, FULL OF GRACE, THAT BY THE ENDING OF THIS LIFE, THE LIFE OF AN UNWILLING; THAT IT SHALL BRING FORTH THE RAFTERS OF OUR HOUSE. A HOUSE FOR OUR GODDESS OF A THOUSAND NAMES. ALDINACH, BELIAL, ASTAROTH, LEVIATHAN, SPHINX, CHIMERA, BELETH, GAIA, VALAC, MALPHAS, BAHAMUT, BEHEMOTH, YŌKAI. ALL THE SAME."

"WE HAIL."

The crowd erupted.

"HAIL.....HAIL.....HAIL....HAIL...."

The voice of the Master quietened but still rang David's ears with steely discomfort.

"All the same. The Great One, full of hope and love, brimming with power, ready and willing to transform this land."

The Master nodded, and a congregation member paced forward, skulking behind the wheel. They took hold of the rope alongside his sibling, wrapping it around their arms and elbows.

"For our writings clearly say that in later times, some will abandon the faith and follow deceiving spirits and things taught by demons. We gave this man the chance to leave us to our work, but he has refused. He has denied himself and his spirit a place in the new world soon to come."

A figure from the shadows emerged, a coiled leather strap wrapped around their hands. Loosening their grip slightly, it unravelled, revealing it completely. Upon the end was a metal buckle, solid and brutal. Peppered across the edges and body of the crop were a dozen or more thumbtacks; their cruel pinpoints pierced the leather, poking through the other side.

The Master spoke verses of the scripture directly from memory. There was no need for reference; these words were firmly imprinted into their minds.

“Blessed is the one who reads aloud the words of this prophecy, and blessed are those who hear and keep what is written in it, for the time is near.”

What he felt next was an explosion. A tremendous and prolonged bending of his limbs. He felt it in his old and weathered knees, in his ankles that had marched a million paces of the beat, in his hands and wrists that had cuffed countless of the guilty.

And then a SNAP.

The belt lashed his exposed stomach, pins first. They perforated his solar plexus, sticking in place momentarily before being torn out with a horrible tug. It scratched and shredded him, drawing scarlet teardrops that cascaded onto his pelvis. A wrenching, ripping render against the heretic.

A howl rang from deep inside him, somewhere he did not know existed; it sent shockwaves of his inner turmoil across the chamber.

The Master spoke once more, the words becoming a fevered rhythmic chant.

“But mark this: There will be terrible times in the last days. People will be boastful, proud, abusive, disobedient, ungrateful, unholy, without love, unforgiving, slanderous, without self-control, brutal, not lovers of the correct; they are treacherous, rash, conceited, lovers of pleasure rather than lovers of God. We have nothing to do with such people. "

His tendons and muscles expanded as the wheel began to turn, his head remaining still. The ropes tugged and tightened.
Fire flowed inside him, burning, scolding as he began tearing at the seams. His screams echoed louder. His very flesh and muscles split and burst, pulling apart like wet and flimsy tissue paper.

Nothing could have prepared him for what he felt at that moment. The sheer essence of torture, a limitless horizon of agony. It was maddening.

Another looping throw of the belt.

A solid THUMP.

This time, it landed buckle first against his ribs, a solid crunch of broken bones snapping and splintering. A mauling sledgehammer of pain bruised and thudded against his exposed lungs inside of him. An immediate welt arose from the crater made on his side, rosy, red and risen.

The Master pointed a bony gloved finger at David.

"But watch yourselves lest your hearts be weighed down with dissipation and drunkenness and cares of this life, and that day come upon you suddenly like a trap."

The mask that covered the Master's face saved David from being spittled upon, such was the venom and bile that the sentence had.

Once more, the wheel turned, and his arms and legs popped from their joints, a repulsive cracking of ligaments and bone. What remained of his teeth clenched together, gnashing and squeaking together, a globule of blood dropped from in between his tightened lips.

The pain was impalpable, immeasurable, and infinite; he could feel himself slipping away, and the darkness of unconsciousness began to take him far away from this agony. The vice-like grip of the ropes started to sink past the first layer of skin, digging and gorging his wrists and ankles.

In a sudden snap, he fell in a heap. The bonds had been released, and the rope knot loosened completely; he crashed to the floor like a ragdoll. His head knocked against the solid ground, an insult to injury.

A cruel series of laughter sang across the echoing hall, the flock, the parishioners delighting in the display of sacrifice ahead of them.

The Master stepped forward and placed a boot on the side of the defeated and limp man in front of them, pressing and prodding, poking at the already broken specimen.

"The Oubliette. A place to forget our foes. A pit, a hole, a gap in the earth itself. This is where the unwilling shall be sent to. This is how we displace our past and move gloriously onto our prosperous future. AND SO WE HAIL."

They shoved him in a sudden jolt with a heavy and unforgiving foot. He sailed and dropped like a stone into the bleak. All to the noise of the chorus line, chanting in unison, a mighty and cruel:

"HAIL.....HAIL.....HAIL....HAIL......"

The chasm took him now.

The emptiness shrouded him as he muttered a breath of words before entering the abyss.

His mantra. His phrase. His epitaph.

"I.....promise.....you....this......"

Chapter 18: Something Wicked This Way Comes

The Master meandered away in solitude, silently slinking through the tangled and winding corridors. Their mind singing, wringing, screaming and thrumming with excitement. Their body barely contained their exuberance at the joyous event soon to come. As they stepped into the darkness, their mind changed into their linchpin.

Their baby boy.

Torn down suddenly.

Removed from this world too soon.

The memories were as cruel as eternal haunting spectres, as vicious as a cancer diagnosis. They recalled this morning, the same as every morning; they woke, anticipating the sound of tiny pitter-pattering footsteps running down the hallway. The gentle and joyous noises of his chuckling, discovering something new to tinker and amuse himself with, but there was silence. Silence for many years now.

They imagined the smell of his hair, the feel of his hand, the warmth of his smile. Now, only bone, ash and cruel memories remained.

His first day of school. So nervous, he cried and bawled thick, sorrowful tears as he left his guardian for the first time. Mopping his face with a soft tissue that was previously crammed in his pocket, he waved a tiny hand at his parent, now weeping as well; their fingers shook with anxiety as he walked through the gate of the school and into the classroom. It was their last memory of him alive.

Dense tears leaked through the gaps of The Master's mask, dropletting on the ground beneath them. Each one a thorn, each one a kidney punch, each one a cruel reminder of their loss in a world so uncaring. That was soon to change. They found themselves once more on the knife's edge of anger and utmost depression; a singular wobble could topple them either way, but this was not the aim. The Master used this state as meditation.

As a prayer to the Holy Goddess, full of grace. And so they walked onwards until they arrived at their penultimate destination.

Opening a wide door within the labyrinthine building, they found themselves in the next sanctum, in front of the next offering. They were almost done. So tantalisingly close. So near and yet so far.

The room softly glowed with the light of brass oil lamps that covered the walls, floor and high ceilings; it revealed three things. A pair of solid and heavy metal gauntlets, like those from a suit of mediaeval armour; they shone, immaculately polished and chromed; inside the gloves, The Master could see they were stuffed, lined with soft blue velvet.

And then a box. Roughly 6 feet by 6, a wooden crate, sturdy and still. From within, they heard a soft slither crawling across the grains of the wood, something dewey and damp. A nestling rattle rang a warning of hidden venom within. Teeth and fangs as sharp as hypodermic needles lined the mouth of it as it crawled uselessly to try and find a hole to slink through. Its slit pupils are as deep and inky black as a trench at the bottom of the ocean, its irises a dull greenish brown, like a dying plant starved of rain.

The Master stood, perching a foot on the lid of the crate. A remorseless and cold-blooded hiss sang from within. With a shoving kick, the top flew open, and the box lay on its side. Revealed now was the beast that formerly lay within. A rattlesnake. Its body is as thick as a weightlifter's triceps, pure rippling scaly muscle. It was long and coiled, spiralling into itself, sprung and ready to snap.

The Master crept slowly forward, crouching low, overseeing the deadly animal with diligent eyes. They picked up the pair of gauntlets and slipped them over their hands, already covered in white gloves, speckled with the browning red of drying blood.

They fit their hands loosely, but they could still control the fingers of the heavy metal implement with ease.

With a piercing hiss and a jostling rattle of the tail, the serpent sent a mortal warning to the towering humanesque figure in front of it; it was ignored absolutely.

The Master lunged forward quickly, grasping at the head of the snake. The beast struck, hitting the solid steel of the armour; it pinged off and recoiled itself. Before it could recover, The Master grabbed again, taking hold of their target. It wriggled and flapped in its tightened metal fist, its grasp firmly around the head of the slithering serpent.

A slight squeeze, the most minor pressure exerted on the sides of its jaw, revealed a series of teeth as sharp and unforgiving as a Venus fly trap. A tiny droplet of yellowing, pale, thick liquid fell onto the crease of the fingers of the guarded hand. The Master imagined this pearl of poison, this vessel of venom holding so much death, so much destruction, a perfect parallel of the world itself. A mirror held up to the face of humanity, unrelenting, unyielding, wild and free. There is no concept of sin or morality, the essence of evil incarnate.

They ran through the sacraments in their mind, the tenets and ideals of their faith, unwavering and holy. Passages flooded their brain, unable for the first time to latch onto a single one in the joy and excitement of the looming event soon to occur.

The snake's mouth was now agape; the Master brought their protected thumb and pointer finger up to the animal's jaws. Grasping it tightly, they flicked their wrist back, wringing the milky pearlescent pinpoint of teeth forward. With the sudden snap, the fangs broke away from the gums, dripping with toxins. The beast's tail flickered wildly, lashing up and down, backwards and forwards, side to side, looping, whipping a frenzy, a whirling dervish of primal pain and anger.

The Master removed the gauntlet from their free right hand by shaking it free; it clanged and clattered unceremoniously against the ground in a heap. They reached for the tail, still curling and twitching in pain. Eventually, they grasped it before putting a solid boot downwards, pinning it to the floor helplessly. They plucked the two needle-like teeth from the floor. As they did, they felt the wet residue of venom sink into the fabric of the cotton glove; it was as warm and sticky as honey harvested from a hive. With the teeth pointed sideways in their finger and thumbs, they kept the creature taught and tight so it could no longer squirm.

They set their sights just above the brown dead skin of the rattle.

Slowly, they pierced the golden brown scaled skin.

Calmly, they slid the teeth through the muscly flesh of the beast itself.

Hitting bone halfway through, they pushed just a little firmer, pushing past and through the other side. The Master felt the life beginning to drain from the suppressed animal in their control and so quickened their pace.

Their other hand, still holding the head of the beast, came downwards to the tail end. The needles passed through the soft jaw and upwards. A return of teeth from where they once belonged but inverted.

A cruel joke, a twist of fate.

The Master plunged the snake's exposed teeth that poked through the body of itself, now through the head and brain of the squirming soul. A perfect circle. A snake that eats its own tail. A story as old as time. Life. Death. Rebirth.

Each one of these is brutal, bloody and painful.

The snake twitched its last sad moments on the floor as The Master watched onwards until there was no more. No more pain. No more suffering. No more sin. An Ouroboros. A deceased mound of flesh in a brutal, bloody, tangled circle.

The beast, the original depiction of evil, lay dead at their feet. No more life left within its bleeding shell.

Elation spread across every inch, every centimetre, within every cell of The Master's body. In these moments of sacrifice, the world was forgotten but never forgiven.

The house was now built. And so they hailed silently to themselves in a corner of their mind.

HAIL..... HAIL......HAIL.... HAIL.....

The foundation, pillars, rafters and roof are constructed, stable and solid.

Now was the time to open the door and let what had been waiting so long to crawl inside. Millenniums spent in rest. Now, soon to be awoken.

Not long now.

Chapter 19: Further Down The Spiral

Jake ran as far and as fast as his legs could carry him.

He haphazardly navigated the eerie abandoned waterworks, sprinting with a swaying flashlight. Every creak and echo in the vast decaying structure kept him moving, determined to bring this horror to an end. He was deep within the palace where the echoes of its industrial past still reverberated, now nothing more than a decaying monument to bygone days.

His footsteps clapped through the cavernous chambers as he ventured deeper into the defunct waterworks. Minute after minute passed, each winding corridor indistinguishable from the last. The rustling of rodents and distant drips of water were now the only other sounds; they made an eerie symphony that echoed deeply.

As he continued, his lungs began to burn at the repeated effort of heaving his footsteps. He slowed, and as he did, the sense of dread began to slowly settle on top of him, a cold, icy blanket. It was as if the building was conspiring against him, shifting and changing, leading him further astray. Panic began to claw at his throat as he realised he was utterly lost in this desolate place, cut out from the outside world. They could be lurking in the shadows, watching his every move, and he would be none the wiser. Since leaving the side of David, he had become the prey in this deadly game of cat and mouse, no longer the hunter; he had become the hunted.

After what felt like seemingly a lifetime, he smelt the scent of extinguished candles, smokey and still. He followed this like a bloodhound seeking out their escaped prisoner. Within moments, his torch settled on a dark room. It was vastly huge, circular and empty of life, yet full of death.

What he saw sent him careening backwards in disgust. A pile of intestines, guts and organs lay on the floor, still and black as cut obsidian.

A colossal golden-furred beast was strung up, hanging from its neck. Its side had been gorged open by some long sharp object. The smell was putrid, like a butcher's shop in the middle of a hot day. He heaved in his mouth, barely keeping down his last meal.

It was then that he heard the drum beat again. A thumping, resonating bass that shook the very foundations he stood upon. It was close. Very close.

In between the dull thuds, he heard footsteps, short but sharp pitter-patters of toes and heels marching forward, a lot more than just one pair. The smell of blood and meat was beginning to subside; it was replaced by the aroma of a thick, almost liquid-like cloud starting to enter the room.

It crept across the floor towards him, bringing the smell of sweet molasses, freshly squeezed citrus, effervescent wood smoke and one other thing he could not place his finger upon a scent from childhood; it could have been icing on a birthday cake, the smell of the plastic of a freshly opened action figure, or maybe the smell of an empty tub of Play-Doh; whatever it was, it gave to him a warm nerve tingling nostalgic flush, a twinkle of goose pimples flew across his arms. It made him smile widely and deeply for the first time in weeks or perhaps even months.

He saw them, marching forwards with a brass gaslamp held upon high, a hooded figure wearing a pearly white mask over their face. It was covered with droplets of dried blood and regal purple sigils, unrecognised but familiar. Behind the first followed five others.

One swung an embellished bronze sphere on the end of a silver chain; it bellowed the sickly sweet smoke permeating his nostrils and bewitching his senses.

One supported a large bass drum with brown leather straps over their broad shoulders; they were noticeably more prominent than the others, and their footsteps thudded in time with each pounding strike of the goat skin. Each thump vibrated his irises, shaking them, sending his vision into rising kaleidoscopic waves; his reality was beginning to shift.

One held a banner aloft, supported by a long silver pole, with an arrow sharp tip. The symbols that covered it mingled and wriggled together. What was once temporarily misunderstood was now fully acknowledged in a thunderbolt of realisation. The everlasting, eternal universe is vast, incalculable and beautiful. It made tears roll down his cheeks at the sheer beauty of it.

One held a tome bound by black leather. It was ancient, dusty and fraying at the edges. The figure holding it chanted and hummed to themselves. The noise was a soft cacophony, a gentle contrast to the thundering drum. Jacob felt that each syllable was a tickling feather caressing and fluttering every fibrous muscle of his body. It sent him into a fit of laughter that controlled every aspect of him. His tears of reverence turned into tears of mirth.

The last held nothing. They creaked forward, slowly walking, shuffled hunched over footsteps that had decades of pain within their bones. They clasped their gloved hands together tightly in a clenched prayer. Remaining silent, the sight of them sent them into a state of absolute terror. Cold sweat burst out from Jacob's pores, and he began to twitch, a body-wide contraction, an ultimate form of paroxysm.

As the crowd moved closer to Jacob, he began to claw at his skin with his trimmed nails; the terror that had overtaken him was too much to bear. Every inch of his being urged and pushed him forward to tear himself apart, to pull himself away, to be reborn somewhere far from here.

Blood ran down his biceps and forearms, his eyelids fluttered open and closed, and his muscles tensed. His lungs felt like they were being filled with concrete; he gasped and begged for breath.

In a rush, a giant gust of wind eradicated the smoke from the room, and the smoking orb was extinguished.

The old and weathered figure walked until he was almost on top of Jacob. Withdrawing a covered needle from his robe, he unsheathed it before plunging it into Jake's carotid artery. An immediate relief. Catching his breath again, his consciousness began to drop at the seams; the black void wavered on the corners of his vision.

The figure that granted him his relief caressed his cheek softly.

A crooked electronic voice buzzed.

"*Oh, how I have missed this. But you know as well as I do, our work always comes first.*"

The figure removed the mask from their face, and Jacob witness the last straw pulled that brought the pillar of hay tumbling down to the ground. He sank into oblivion.

His father.

Bryan Williams.

A ghost of times past, well and truly here.

Solid.

Alive.

"Hello, Son. Welcome. You're home now. Just in time and not a minute too late."

Chapter 20: Six Feet Under

Time sank to a complete halt.

CORNUCOPIA

In this dimly lit underbelly of an abandoned building, David found himself trapped in what seemed like an endless nightmare, a place where forgotten horrors lingered; his only companions were the moss-covered stone walls and the damp trickle of an infinite stream.

He couldn't help but feel the oppressive weight of solitude. The rock walls seemed to close in on him, suffocating him with a sickening sense of helplessness.

His mangled body ached and burned in horrible pain; his fresh flesh wounds sang a song of despair and anguish. He was a lump.

A useless sack of unmoving muscle, struggling to cling to the edges of consciousness, the pain only moments away from sending him flying backwards into himself, back into the bleak recesses of his mind.

Despite the darkness and despair surrounding him, he refused to give in to hopelessness. His determination to see an end to this was the only fire that remained.

Starting from his head, he began to study his wounds. Before he could move his right arm, a lightning bolt of pain ran through his shoulder. With his weaker left arm, he reached over and felt his body with bruised fingers.

An unnatural jutting edge had formed on his upper back. His shoulder was dislocated, possibly broken and shattered. He wouldn't know until......

Grabbing a hold of the bony bump, he heaved with all of his might.

POP

He screamed from somewhere deep within himself as the cartilage slipped tentatively back into place.

His arm and hand, still ablaze in mind-wracking agony, felt his mouth. A gap had been formed, a vacant hole where a tooth once lived. The nerve had been severed and snapped; it sent a wave of electric brute force that jostled every inch of him.

Feeling a cold wind blow against his bare chest, he buttoned his shirt as he shivered, cold and helpless.

As he did, he felt the once warm but now cold blood covering him. It has begun to congeal and harden; the gashes and scratches were a cruel accent mark on his already defeated body.

He then meticulously examined the cavernous walls, looking for any sign of weakness or vulnerability.

The pit was pitch black; he could barely see his fingers in front of him. His training kicked in as he reached for his flashlight but found it was long gone. What had not gone was his ancient digital watch, now with a giant crack on its face. He pressed the "LIGHT" button, hoping, praying that it still functioned. And with a faint green glow, the walls were illuminated.

He breathed a sigh of relief that was snuffed out as soon as it had arrived. As the walls lit his surroundings, he realised the pit was more profound than he had initially thought, and the walls were seemingly sheer.

Knowing he couldn't rely on anyone, he assessed his only options.

Live or die.

I promise you this.....

He remembered a basic survival training he had received decades ago, the importance of staying calm. Taking a few deep breaths, he examined the pit's walls more closely, searching for any irregularities or possible footholds.

With unwavering determination, he found a small ledge that could serve as a starting point for an escape.

The first toe hold slipped, and the wet walls would not give him his salvation easily. A further attempt resulted in a bashed knee that he barely felt over the other pains writhing through his body.

Anger took hold now. He removed his shoes and tried again, hooking his hairy toes onto the damp rock, gaining any possibility of purchase.

Inch by a painful inch, the cold sweat on his brow began to mix with the dirt and grime from the pit walls, masking his face with the dust and muck.

After what felt like an eternity, so many pained arm stretches, hand clasps, and leg pulls, he finally reached the top of the pit. Exhausted and covered in dirt, he hoisted himself over the edge and collapsed onto the ground above.

Tiny droplets of blood trickled from his mouth, and his shirt, now a bloody and ripped rag, barely clung to his chest.

He rested now for what he intended to be the shortest of moments. It was not to be.

He huffed a last breath before unconsciousness finally drifted him away. He imagined he was falling asleep on the battered sofa in

Henry Lloyd's ramshackle and dirty apartment after a long and painful night of booze to nullify the sorrow of the day that had passed.

"I promise you this......"

Chapter 21: The Meeting Of Minds

The end was here.

The beginning was about to occur.

A vast cylindrical metal tower, hundreds of feet tall and wide, began to power up.

Something inside of it stirred; a howling vortex of rushing water cascaded and muddled together within.

The congregation spread around the metallic behemoth, watching and listening. Jacob was on the floor, unmoving, unconscious.

The Master arrived, appearing high above on a metallic strut attached to the tower. They spoke loud and true with an electric whine of alteration.

'My siblings, prostrate yourselves, even as I do pray to the Holy Mother to protect and assist me in the labours we will undertake."

The Master pressed a large blue button that rested on a hoisted cable by their side. A clunking whir jostled the scaffold that surrounded the tower. After a few moments, arriving on a chain-link track, a cart. It was itself the size of a small house, and it was packed to the brim. Full of a silvery-white chalky sludge.

"For this, my siblings is our Soma. Our sustenance. Our Saviour. A product of the evils of society itself now turned inwards. Used for our benefit. Used for salvation. Used to wipe this world clean."

The Master once more pressed the button, and it tipped into the whirling vortex of fluid that was now filling the gigantic tower of water.

The congregation sang.

"HAIL..... HAIL..... HAIL.....HAIL"

"Vide. Aude. Vole. Tache. To know. To dare. To will. To remain silent. These are the powers of our Holy Mother, the being with a thousand names. The wings of an eagle signify air. The horns of a Bull signify earth. The body of a lion signifies fire. The tail of a serpent signifies water. The head of a woman signifies the holy spirit itself. She teaches us that to learn to will is to learn how to exercise dominion. But to exert power, you must first know; for will power applied to folly and sin is madness, death, and hell."

"HAIL....HAIL....HAIL....HAIL"

Jacob began to rouse; his fingers twitched, and his eyes began to open.

"For as it was in the last days of Rome, the holy overcame the heathens. The mighty and righteous overcame the vindictive and the vile. The tallest towers become the easiest to topple; those lowest down shall soon be uplifted.

"HAIL....HAIL....HAIL....HAIL"

Jacob now looked up and saw the figure upon high. As he did, he saw an industrial map, tangled and messy in its elaborate lines. What was clear, though, was that this old system, although barely standing, was still operational. It was still linked to every house and every area of the city. Millions upon millions of buildings are still hooked into the rusted lines of this old building. He also saw the enormous upturned vat, still leaking pearlescent liquid into the tower.

The realisation struck him.

This was the end game.

This was the finishing line.

"I see our sibling has awoken. Jacob. Stand and join us."

Jake stood slowly. He scanned each figure carefully, watching them with caution.

"Fear not, child. You are here now. You are with your family."

The robed one nearest to him once again removed their mask.

Jake had hoped it was a figment of his imagination.

It was not to be.

It was his father.

He was 20 years older, a fading fragment of what he once was, but it was his father.

"How I have missed you son."

Tears streamed down each of their faces. A slow and sorrowful sob coughed up from the bottom of their souls, once again reunited after far too long.

Bryan embraced his son for the first time in decades as the congregation proceeded forward, watching in silence. The first had been revealed.

Jake could see, almost imperceptibly, a shadow in the corner of the vast room. It drew closer.

The second masked figure, a muscular and well-built shadow, removed their visage. The handcuffed man who was at the bar was now free; Jacob recognised him in an instant. He could see a black eye beginning to form, and a bloody red lip swelled on his jaw. He took his right index finger and placed it into his mouth.

He swirled it around, his eyes squinted, revealing a wince of pain occurring within him. He removed his finger from his mouth; it dripped a red globule of blood. He moved forwards onto Jacob, still in his warm paternal embrace, and with it drew a single scarlet stripe from his high widow's peak down onto the tip of his nose. A blood offering, an olive branch, a sign of respect and unison. The second had been revealed.

The shadow in the corner came into clearer view; it crept slowly and quietly. It looked like it was in a deep state of pain. It was David. Making slow eye contact with Jacob, he raised a finger to his lips. He limped and struggled. Something had hurt him deeply, almost to the point of death. His face was battered, bruised, scratched and torn. His clothes barely clung to him; they were strands of scarlet red rags attached only by the scabbed blood on his torso.

The third, a large burly physique in their outline, unlatched a hook from their neck, and their covering fell to the floor. Jacob knew this person; the questions rolled around in his mind, yet to be answered.

Lee Harper. District Attorney of the state. Jacob had seen him countless times in the courtrooms and meetings of the state. A physically colossal man, his presence and sheer size made Jacob aware that although he was more than twice his age, the weathered DA would still be able to easily dominate him. His giant right hand, as large as a bear's paw, was held open, palm outstretched. He lifted his arm high into the heavens, fingers splayed, dancing in the cool night air of this wasteland. He wiggled them, and they danced and wavered, conjuring something invisible, invoking an ancient thing, once forgotten, now recalled. As he did, he muttered something.

It was a language he did not comprehend; it sounded ancient, strenuous, and warped. It was full of love, acceptance and respect.

He placed his hand on Jacob's left shoulder, shuddering with fear.

He spoke once more.

“The curse is on the house of the wicked but blesses the home of the righteous.
We mock proud mockers but show favour to the humble and oppressed.
The wise inherit honour, but fools get only shame.”

As he finished, he made solid and unbreaking eye contact with Jacob, his pupils narrowed as if trying to look directly into the deepest recesses of his soul; he sized him up, evaluated, and then gave a solid, reassuring nod.

“The thing to always remember in these troubling times, Jacob, is one simple thing.”

His hand was removed from Jake's shoulder, and he pointed his index finger, as wide and thick as a sausage link, as he drew an invisible line across the officer's face, from the bottom of his left eye socket, over his nose, and onto the top of his right eye socket.

“THIS TOO SHALL PASS”

He walked away, his footsteps thudding on the solid floor, as he started to sing to himself.

“Now the sun wants to rise as brightly
As if nothing terrible had happened during the night.

CORNUCOPIA

The misfortune happened only to me,
But the sun shines equally on everyone."

He rocked and swayed, his voice sending him into a trance. He joined the group once more, the third one revealed.

"You must not fold the night into yourself.
You must bathe it in eternal light.
A little lamp has gone out in my tent.
I must greet the joyful light of the world."

The group began to hum as he continued, arms held high aloft in a salute to the Holy one above.

"Now I see why, with such dark flames
Your eyes flash at me at certain moments.
O eyes, it was as if in a single glance
You could concentrate your full power."

The group of robed figures now all started to sing.

"Yet I didn't realise because mists were floating around me,
Woven by a blinding fate,
That your beam of light was ready to be sent home,
To the place from which all beams emanate."

A masked figure, still in the background, sang the next verse alone.

"You wanted to tell me with your light:
We wish to stay near forever.
But that was taken away by fate.
Look straight at us because soon we will be far away.
What to you are only eyes in these days,
In the nights to come will be only stars."

Jacob recognised the voice but almost refused to acknowledge the information until it was confirmed when they removed their mask. Kevin Donne, Blood Spatter Analyst and previous Chief of the County Coroner's office. He walked towards Jake, still in his father's embrace, dropped to one knee, and bowed. The crowd continued.

“In this weather, in this windy storm,
I would never have sent the children out.
They have been carried off,
I wasn't able to warn them.”

Kevin slid his finger across the dirt-covered floor and moved forward onto Jacob. He drew a solid blackish-brown line of grime and grit that ran from the bottom of his right eye socket, over his nose and onto the top of his left eye socket. The group's voice became louder.

“In this weather, in this gale,
I would never have let the children out.
I feared they sickened:
Those thoughts are now in vain.”

Kevin moved away and joined the group once more, the fourth now revealed.

“In this weather, in this storm,
I would never have let the children out,
I was anxious they might die the next day:
Now anxiety is pointless.”

The Master proceeded down a metallic catwalk high above and entered a cage wired to the side of the tower. Pressing a button on the inside, it began its descent downwards.

“In this weather, in this windy storm,

I would never have sent the children out.
They have been carried off,
I wasn't able to warn them."

The Master now reached the ground, the cage door rattled wide open as they marched forwards, head bowed and arms crossed. They walked to the remaining masked person.

They bowed to each other in perfect unison, and as they arose, they clasped a hold of their masks, revealing themselves together.

The crowd sang louder and prouder still.

"In this weather, in this gale, in this windy storm,
they rest as if in their mother's house:
frightened by no storm,
sheltered by the Hand of God."

Jacob could see now David was ambling closer. He could see that David, too, had recognised the unmasked congregation. David's eyes, although bruised and swollen, were wide open in disbelief.

David took another slow crouching step, but his weight and the rusted decaying metal betrayed him; a mighty groaning creak from the floor revealed him to the crowd. The four revealed kept their steely gaze on Jacob. The remaining two turned to David.

The hoods still covered their heads as they walked towards David; he shuffled back towards the corner, a trapped rat, unable to run.

"You live." One said.

Their voice was old and shattered. A cold memory of the past jolted through David. A once warm voice is now frozen and piercing. A voice of a teacher scorned, a sensei betrayed. They lifted their hood as David shook his head in denial.

His mentor. His tutor. His father that taught him the ropes. It was Henry. Alive and in the flesh, but barely.

It was decades since he last saw him and showed it deeply. His brow, which once was wrinkled and furrowed, was covered in liver spots, and his hair, once as fleeting and soft as dying candle smoke, was now absent. His deep and soulful brown eyes were still hidden by an untamed bushel of eyebrow hair, wirey, pointed and wild. His now completely white moustache had been stained a muddy brown by the decades of nicotine; it decorated his mouth, which was now frowning intently.

“David. You promised me. You broke a promise. That makes me upset.”

“First things first, Henry.”

The tempo, enunciation, tone and accent of the voice were immediately recognisable.

David shook his head in denial.

It was the Captain’s voice.

Terri Cauldwell, with her familiar southern drawl tamed by time, tide and practice. A smooth and silken timbre, now full of hatred and desire.

Her glassy blue eyes pierced Davids, and her sandy blonde hair was tied in a tight ponytail.

She was the definition of a perfect leader. It had taken her 10 years to get to this role as the Master; it was not without heartache, betrayal, and sexism. She had surpassed this with grace and utmost devotion to the Holy Mother, full of Grace. Steely and solid, she is a born authority. Highly organised, motivated and driven by her faith. Beyond anything, she would do anything for her son, now long gone, a memory of the past. Cut down too soon by an uncaring world, unwilling to help and not yet ready for change.

But she would no longer wait.

Enough time had passed.

The world needed to change.

She was the one to make it happen.

Chapter 22: Orpheus & Eurydice

“First things first”

The sentence made David's blood run cold.

"Brother Rho, come forward."

The bruised and battered bartender from Vincenzo's shuffled forward towards The Master like a scalded child.

"Your contribution to our cause has been commendable. You supplied us with a temporary home for our teachings, a storage area for the Soma, soon to sweep this world clean."

He knelt on one knee, a genuflection for his faith.

"You provided us with an unwilling vessel to act as the catalyst impelling the spirit of air, the eagle, whose very wings flew too close to the sun, a necessary removal, split into two pieces to ensure the temple's foundations are grounded."

He drew an invisible sigil with his hand over his face and body, his middle finger pressed against his thumb firmly.

"You have provided us with a willing vessel to act as the catalyst impelling the spirit of the earth, the Bull, who skins himself clean from their mortal shell, ready to be reborn. You have provided us with a reverent vessel to act as the catalyst for fire, the Lion, whose very flesh shall be hung, pierced and eaten by the congregation. For it is in this act that we shall overcome the vicious and malicious, the ones with evil thoughts and brutish intentions."

The bartender wept.

"Your task, however, the most important so far - the spirit of water encapsulated within a denier....."

She pointed a skinny digit at David, her finger wagging with barely suppressed rage.

"An outsider, a stranger, an uncaring and unwilling worshipper of sin. A drunkard, following orders blindly without care for the world around him."

Terri, the Captain, the Master, held her face in her hands and screamed.

A wail of endless pain kept within her for decades was now released.

"My boy. My poor boy. I called him Adam. You remember him, don't you?"

David did remember him, painfully and full of regret.

It was ten and a half years ago.

A school shooting. It made the national news, covered by all major television networks nationwide and worldwide.

A tragedy.

A senseless ending of life, all in the name of another hopeless soul wanting to be heard, to be recognised, to be understood endlessly.

David was there that day.

A madman entered the building.

A lunatic spouting insane rhetoric.

Another Mark David Chapman, another Ted Kaczynski, another David Berkowitz, another Eric Harris and Dylan Klebold - all are wanting but in their minds NEEDING those elusive fifteen minutes of fame.

He held the teacher hostage in front of the screaming and clamouring school students, waving his Desert Eagle carelessly underneath the cold sectional ceiling of the classroom.

He was the product of an uncaring society; he had been overlooked for too long, and now was his time to be put on the map for eternity.

A misplaced, abused and broken cog screaming for help, he had been ignored, scorned and abused.

No longer.

No fucking longer.

It all came to an end that day.

David remembers entering the situation, gun held high.

“PUT YOUR GUN DOWN, NOW.”

The madman, as yet unnamed, refused; his irises were wide open, an endless inky black. His gun was now beginning to aim wildly, no longer at his hostage but at the wailing children attempting to take cover underneath their feeble wooden tables.

“WE CAN TALK THIS THROUGH. COME ON, JUST LISTEN TO ME.”

The gun holder's neck muscle twitched. Something deep within him shifted.

He began to change his aim slowly to the person bargaining with him.

David noticed the change.

David's left eye closed.

David's right eye looked directly down at the iron sight of his pistol.

David did not hesitate.

It was his life now at stake. A gamble he did not wish to place a bet upon.

He fired.

As he did, the man also released a shot, firing wildly into the crowd.

An ear-piercing cacophony of screams rang out from the crowd. A cry of the desperate.

A song of the damned.

The bullets struck home.

One in the head of the assailant, his skull exploded across the crudely drawn finger paintings behind him.

The other penetrated the heart of a child, piercing their aorta, splitting their vital organ into a dozen bloody pieces.

A purely innocent bystander, a brown-haired cherub cut down from life too soon.

In the chaos, the remaining people ran for their lives, unaware that the worst had already happened to another.

Over the upcoming hours, his team tried desperately to suppress it from leaking to the public, at least for now, but the damage had been done.

David was questioned endlessly by the press; they were eager and bloodthirsty to report the latest travesty that had landed in their laps.

Within minutes, a hundred parents were at the scene, each weeping deeply. At that moment, he saw in their eyes the primordial and profound relief of saviour that David had delivered them as they were reunited with their kin.

In the crowd was the Captain, Terri Cauldwell.

Her child did not come forward.

Hers was the soul that had been slain.

David remembered.

Deeply, he carried this burden of death.

In the upcoming days, Terri was questioned, barraged with a million questions that had no answers.

David himself was also interviewed. He continued, as he always did. A man of duty, he only did what he thought was correct and just.

And so it was.

Within a blink of days, the media's attention was drawn to another tragedy.

Another product of the horrid cornucopia that the public held so firmly upon.

A society of sin, a living of the languid, a miasma of misery.

David's eyes were wide open in understanding. His vision wavered and began to shift as grey smoke entered the room.

"Brother Rho, your final task was unsuccessful. But there is still time for redemption."

The Captain, The Master, withdrew a familiar firearm from a deep pocket on her robe; it was David's sidearm.

She passed it to the kneeling familiar.

He held the gun and put his finger on the trigger as he placed the weapon in his mouth, in a gap where a tooth once resided.

He spoke, his words muffled with cold steel in between his lips.

"The serpent has once again betrayed us, but no longer shall we let it control us with its sins. And so onto the waiting arms of the goddess, I offer my own life as an offering to bring forth new hope into this world."

The hammer of the revolver clicked back, and the trigger was pulled.

BANG.

The bartender lay dead on the floor of the room, enormous, broad and circular.

One shot.

One kill.

The Captain, The Master, nodded in approval as David removed his glance from the scene of brutality.

She spoke.

“And so my siblings, an ultimate sacrifice. Removal of life for another. A believer for a sinner. Our Brother Rho now lies within our Holy Mother's arms, full of grace. A balance of the eternal scales. A cosmic reckoning.”

Terri Cauldwell began to move towards the unmoving corpse.

She held her head upwards as if willing a holy uproar of rain to cascade upon her. She spread her arms far and wide by her sides, imagining she was catching the painful teardrops of the goddess about to inhabit this earth.

She thought, “If only I were to be present for the welcoming…. Such a shame…..”

Chapter 23: The Beginning Of The End

"Grand Hierophant Theta"

The Captain, the Master, spoke to Bryan Williams, whose face was still nuzzled in the shoulder of his son. He slowly stepped backwards, his hand lingering on his young boy's face.

He turned to look at The Master, who now held the revolver that ended the life of Brother Rho, the bartender.

"As you are aware, with a welcoming also comes a departure. As one door opens, another closes. I saved your life that day. I kept the blood from pouring out of your neck. I took you under my wing and welcomed you into our faith. You have repaid your debt a thousandfold. You allowed us access to the soma. You gave us the sacred ingredients, the holy formula, the elixir of death, taken from the heathens of this world, now ready to use against them."

David saw now that the whirring of the water tower was making the towering behemoth wobble. The effort of the machinery clunked and clacked against the mixing of the fluid with the dusty white combination of powders entering into the system. Smoke started to bellow from between the seams of the colossal cylinder, a thin fog of silvery white destruction.

“Now is the time for our ultimate sacrifice. Both are welcoming invitations. Yours to bring a new sibling, your blood, into our fold.”

The Master, the captain, passed the loaded revolver to Bryan.

His hands shook as he knew what was to come.

“My sweet son. I was always with you, even though I was in the shadows. My every thought was for you. You are the one to carry forward our message, our aim, and our goal. Parting this world to welcome another pure and free of sin is now your task. Leaving you again fills me with such sweet sorrow.”

He aimed at his temple, and the barrel of the gun sunk in between his wrinkled skin.

BANG.

One shot.

One kill.

This time, it is permanent and unmistakable.

Bryan Williams, the Grand Hierophant, lay on the floor, his brain and skull fragments splattered across his son's face.

The Master, the captain, moved forward and plucked the hot revolver from the ground with her white-gloved skinny hands.

“Now is the final push. The final descent.”

She fished an object from a deep pocket in her cloak. A small metallic keyfob with one solid green button, it pulsated an effervescent, vibrant glow. It screamed the message:

“GREEN MEANS GO.”

She passed the button to Jacob as she muttered to herself a quiet prayer.

“And so, the torch has been passed. Our new sibling is now tasked with enacting our final will.”

The Master, the captain, held the revolver against her left breast bone, aiming directly at her heart.

“The last piece shall now be placed. We welcome her now; our Holy Mother, full of grace, shall now be awoken. For as it is written, the meek shall inherit this earth; the last of days are now upon the heathens, the brutal, the evil-doers. For them, it will be such a shame.....”

BANG.

One shot.

One kill.

She fell in a heap as she breathed her last breath, full of holy blood and vengeful spittle.

David saw now that Jacob remained still, his eyes and body unmoving.

Fight, flight, fawn or freeze.

Typically, narcissists tend towards fighting. They are controlling people with anger issues. There was no shred of rage within Jacob's body, only a bottomless pit of sorrow.

Fawning is for people-pleasers, co-dependent, identity confused and without boundaries. No. Not now. Not here.

Flight was not an option. He was forced to stay and confront what had just happened before him, right here, right now.

To freeze is reserved for people who are struggling to make decisions, they are often emotionally numb and tend to dissociate. This is where Jacob now stood. As still and as wavering as a marble statue.

The congregation now cried out in worship. A vibrant hum. An endless buzz. A soul-shattering song.

Jacob’s finger wavered across the button.

He imagined the endless pain of this world. The countless uncaring souls who have created this pit of misery in which they call life.

Nihilists.

Nepotists.

Sinners.

HEATHENS.

David could see within him the knife's edge of indecision sweeping across Jacob's face. It only lasted a few moments before turning into a languid yet intentional smile.

Jacob moved towards the corpse of his father; he peeled away the mask from his bloody scalp.

He moved towards the Master, the captain, and plucked the revolver from her cold, dead hand.

Jacob spoke now, his voice full of reverence, his soul exploding with purpose.

"Let us join together, my siblings……"

David's soul inverted, bringing a solid shakiness of dread in his voice.

"No, kid, don't do this….."

Jacob ignored him and proceeded.

"Let us become one as we welcome this new world together."

David's stomach turned, dreading what was to come.

Jacob waved his hand, inviting the remaining congregation to come forward.

They complied, echoing their approval in an ear-shattering:

"HAIL.....HAIL.....HAIL....HAIL...."

Kevin Donne, Lee Harper and Henry Lloyd stood together, watching their new Master take charge.

Ready and willing.

"Together we stand."

Jacob's face shifted in an instant.

"Divided, you fall"

BANG.

BANG.

Two picture-perfect shots rang true, perforating the skulls of the DA and the Coroner.

They fell to the floor, jaws wide open in shock and despair.

He dropped the button and smashed it underneath the heel of his right foot. As he did, the titanic whirr of the water tower stopped dead. The smoke settled into the giant canister, ceasing its deadly path of destruction.

Jacob's glance turned to David.

"My sibling."

He turned the gun barrel forward towards him, aiming directly at David's forehead.

With a quick flick of his wrist, he turned the revolver in his hands, twisting it so that the grip was pointed towards David. An olive branch. An offering. A gift of the holy.

"This next one, I believe, is yours…."

David walked forward.

Gently, yet firmly, he took the gun from Jacob's hand.

He felt the solid weight of it as it entered his palm.

David looked upon the only remaining survivor. His mentor, his sensei, his teacher.

With pure and unending vitriol, he aimed.

"I promise you this….."

BANG.

Prologue: After The Goldrush

In the upcoming hours, dozens, if not hundreds, of television and radio crews were on the scene, reporting the events worldwide.

It was probably a leak from one of the several officers now flooding the outskirts of the old and decrepit water works, desperately trying in vain to wrap up what had almost occurred.

David and Jacob ambled forward, hand in hand, elbow over shoulder; together, they were brothers in arms.

The paparazzo captured a million flashing photographs of them as the police on the scene barely kept the snapping vultures at bay.

David and Jacob remained silent throughout. They hobbled together and entered an ambulance through the wide open backdoor before being closed, a solid slam.

The flashing blue and red light flickered brightly as the alarm rang a siren's song. It began its slow journey back into the city. As it did, David's glance poked through the one-way glass; the peak of a hill revealed the city horizon. They were back once more. Iroquois Point. Back to where mother and son were reunited in death: Naomi & Michael Young.

Something in David's head shifted.

He knocked on the ambulance wall heavily as he yelled a demand to cease. His fists stung with pain whilst doing so.

He cried a solid request.

"STOP!"

The vehicle did so, screeching to a halt, and within a few moments, the rear door was open, the driver surveying the mangled bodies of the officers within.

"Everything ok back here?"

David nodded as he tugged at Jacob's sleeve, inviting him to follow his lead.

"Fine, thanks. We'll walk from here."

The driver blinked in disbelief, surveying the wounds of the men, each deep in agony, both physical and mental.

They would live, but it would not be without pain and anguish.

David and Jacob shuffled out slowly, limping as their eyes adjusted to the rising sun that was beginning to poke over the horizon.

The ambulance driver shrugged.

"Your call boss."

He closed the rear door before re-entering the vehicle. It idled for the briefest of moments before driving away, heading towards the metropolis in the distance.

David sat on the dusty desert hilltop, his back pressing against a mesquite tree for support. He invited Jacob to do the same.

They sat together in total silence, hand in hand, as they watched the sun come up, spreading its life-giving rays across the horizon.

The quiet music from the town never ceased, not even for the faintest of moments.

It was them that had changed and not the place. It remained the same, always.

CORNUCOPIA

A vista of neon lights advertising all manners of delights: Dancers, Karaoke, Cheap Drinks, Now Performing: That Band that you'll never remember the name of but had a Top 10 hit in the late 1970s.

Every day.

Every moment.

24/7 - 365.

They rested in each other's arms, their eyelids closed in slumber.
The ambulance's siren rang out from far away; the noise flew across the city.
It was not for them.
It was for someone else in this city that never sleeps.

THE END.

Printed in Great Britain
by Amazon

36690933R00111